WASN'T IT ONLY YESTERDAY

To: Mrs Z...
Hope you enjoy this
Book! God Bless
8/2/07

WASN'T IT ONLY YESTERDAY

by

Mario G. Fumarola
Illustrations by Robert Cimbalo

The Ethnic Heritage Studies Center
Utica College

CONTENTS

Preface 19

Second Floor Rear
Different Times

The Feast 25

We'll Call Him Tony
They All Came Scrambling
Tony is Found
Fridone Hustling . . . Free Bottle
Gnumariedi . . . last glass
Phone Call . . . Chewing Gum
Winding the Clock . . . Funeral

The Economy 83

Barbeque Cop
Lunch Pail
Bean Picking . . . Summer Job
The Game . . . The Boss
Fridone's Acceptance
Full Tray . . . Finocchio's Dilemma
The Pig Could Do It
The Fight . . . The Stop Sign

The Neighborhood   131

Turk The Lebanese . . . . PFC Club
Starry night . . . E-Mail
Dentist . . . Chicken Store
Wine Making
The Clothes Line . . . The Brownstone
The Scissors . . . Fresh fish
Porch versus Stoop
Cigars and Fingers

The Requiem   189

Carlo's Identification
A Thousand Words . . . Ash Wednesday
Intro to Paulie
Carmen's and Espresso

Epilogue   227

The Visitation
White Water Basin
Winter Fig Tree

This Narrative is dedicated to the living and dead souls of . . .

A crowd . . . a huge crowd . . . was gathering in front of the Wizard of Oz's drawn blue

curtain . . . *Silence!!!* he roared . . . and a few seconds afterward . . .

Roared again . . . *Silence!* the crowd became silent . . . *Who speaks for this wretched mass of humanity?*

He asked. *I do!* Someone answered. *What is your name?*

My name is Tony . . . . Who are you? the Wizard asked . . . *I am nobody!* said Tony

Who are all those people behind you? Tony quickly looked over his shoulder and then

back at the blue curtain and the direction of that booming voice and said . . .

Well that's Paulie and there's Donetta and there is Fridone and Finnocchio and

my mother and my father . . . my brothers . . . my two sons from the back porch . . .

All my aunts and uncles and cousins from Catherine Street.

The folks from Goomba Joe's and the feast . . .
the Jimmy Western bean picking gang . . .

My first grade class . . . the people with lint in their hair
who worked at the Oneida Knitting

Mills . . . Miss's Bailey fifth grade class . . . the coffee
drinkers from Carmen's and the

Florentine . . . Mr. Lux . . . the shoeless women that follow
the statues of saints . . . saying the

Rosary . . . the lady with the push cart . . . La Banda
Rossa . . . Patsy the Chicken Man . . .

Enough! Enough! Roared the Wizard and then asked
Tony *What do they want?*

Tony replied . . . *I want God to Bless them.*

All of them?? he asked. *All of them* Tony replied

The good, the bad and the ugly, all of them?? . . . again . . .
all of them Tony repeated

And Tony added . . . *I want God to Bless all of them . . .*

Bless 'em all . . . Bless 'em all . . . the long the short and
the tall . . .

There is a lotta junk in there !!! said the voice
behind the curtain . . .

Tony eyes hooded and his nostril's flared just a bit . . .
he took a deep breath . . .

And simply replied . . . *there is no junk in there* . . .

Whadda ya talk 'bout Tony??? I see lots of junk in there
said the Wizard . . .

Tony's reply was now in a strained pitch . . . he said . . .

There is no junk in there!!!

You are wrong!!! roared the Wizard . . . *and furthermore I
won't bless them!!!*

Tony became visibly angry . . .

He took three steps toward the curtain and in a voice
that sounded more like a hiss

his normal raspy voice . . . he told the curtain . . .
I don't want you to Bless them . . .

I want God to bless them! . . .

*You Wizard . . . are like me . . . a fictional character . . .
just paper and ink . . .*

But NOT these guys behind me . . .

*They are real . . . they laughed . . . cried . . . sang . . .
loved . . . hated . . . dreamed and wished . . .*

And they are NOT junk . . . I'm asking God to bless them all

The long, the short and the tall . . .

The good, the bad and the ugly . . .

All of 'em

Tutti !!!

In his old (older) age,
when Tony would dine out,
he would order a Sambucca as an after dinner drink . . .

and would always remind the waiter/waitress not to forget
to float the three coffee beans in the liquor . . .

He would jokingly tell anyone around him that
by doing so,
it made him feel Italian . . .
should a curious waiter/waitress inquire why or look
confused.

Tony would say,
"It is an Italian custom,
the beans represent the past, present and future."

*Mike and Mintaha speaking in their backyard somewhere
in east Utica . . . circa 1945*

'Ya Mike, our uncle the pear has given rich beautiful fruit

*without a spot for the thirty-three years we have been
married.
And all we do for him is bless him and fill the bushels.
And the*

*plum next to him is weak and we take the worms
from his roots*

every year and he doesn't recover.'

From WIND OF THE LAND by Eugene Paul Nassar

Acknowledgements

I have been advised that an acknowledgement is proper, justifiable and needed.

Two things come to mind . . . the floating coffee beans and my magnificent 'umbrella-pruned' pear tree.

The first coffee bean is my *'only yesterday'* past and my past is like the tap root of the pear tree that slowly drives itself deeper and deeper into the earth. The end of tap root is farthest away from the smallest bud . . . leaf . . . or branch that sits at the very top of the tree, reaching for and following the sunlight. Who is to say it is not all one . . . not all connected . . . not dependent on each other??? Who is to say that is not so??

The past is Pietro and Chiara (Di Risio) Fumarola and two of their three sons. My father left all of his family in the *old country.* My mother's older brothers, Joseph and Michael, her sisters, Grazia De Angelo and Lucia DeBernardis are a part of the *American* root base.

What makes an oak tree so strong? Maybe if we think of the oak's tree root base as an inverted pyramid we can sense an answer to that question.

I acknowledge and thank my past.

With the second coffee bean, the present is what I can see, smell, feel, touch, hear. The part of the pear tree above the earth.

The "present" is my wife, Mary Ann Lewek Fumarola. A patient and understanding woman, a good wife, a good mother, a good partner . . . a good woman. Also my sons, Peter and Raymond, my daughter Colette and her husband, Steve Huber. They have in one way or another contributed. This is the pear tree above the ground but it remains connected to the root base.

With the second coffee bean I also wish to acknowledge two others, outside the twenty-chromosomes of the tap root. They are the illustrator (Robert Cimbalo) and the mentor/advisor (Eugene Nassar).

Mr. Cimbalo's works have always been "fascinating" to me . . . at times driving me into deep dark thoughts of life and understanding and meanings . . . and . . . At other times, making me feel as giddy as a kid coming home from a Saturday matinee. Bob (whose art work will speak for itself) often told me, "I must remain true to the text."

This dedication to his work and East Utica and to the text, forced me . . . maybe even ordered me . . . to remain true to the characters . . . as I see them . . . and then again what is truth? Bob also saw something in a little piece I did and encouraged me to continue. Where does something like this really start and take a life of its own, as did this WIOY??

Eugene P. Nassar, a third string tailback a zillion years ago, who went to college and other colleges . . . went to study in England . . . to travel Europe with another artist . . . became an authority on Ezra Pound . . . And who took the time to read this narrative.

A while back Bob kind of said, "I like some of this stuff, why don't you take a shot at a book? I did give it a shot . . . and shot and reloaded and shot and reloaded. Finally, Bob said to me "Let Gene look at it!" . . . . Would he? Yes he did. The answer in a nutshell was: "Go with it!!" Thank you gentleman.

The third coffee bean . . . the future . . . the uppermost part of the pear tree that looks to the blue sky in the day and the stars at night. The future.

I officially acknowledge four buds very close to the top, my grandchildren: Chiara Huber . . . my mother's name . . . who is bright . . . and very inquisitive . . . Mia Huber . . . Mia means mine in Italian . . . look into this little girl's eyes and you'll know why . . . John Ernest Huber . . . a strong solid name . . . John . . . he is all that a boy his age should be . . . especially to his Pops . . . And finally Little Anna Mae . . . all of my life I believed nothing was beautiful at birth . . . Until I saw this baby . . . The seed for this narrative germinated when I sang to them an old rope-skipping ditty . . . *To buy a pickle.*

These kids bring me a happiness I neither earned nor deserve. Their actions . . . expressions . . . questions and responses . . . overwhelm me.

I acknowledge them because they are the blossoms of spring (La Prima Vera) because they are a part of me . . . And their time will come . . . for a week or ten days my pear tree is pure white in its blossom coat . . . from afar . . . and standing alone . . . it looks like a giant flower . . . soon lingering March and April breezes will tug the petals loose . . . one at a time . . . the petals will look like large snow flakes floating and spiraling to earth . . . and in time may nourish roots.

I want them to know a little bit about Pops . . . Catherine Street . . . A stair case that rose out of the darkness up to a double hung window and bright sunlight . . . a cold water flat in a brownstone that was warm in the winter . . . a different time.

Preface

Second Floor Rear

Different Times

Second-floor Rear

Sixteen steps . . . a spindle railing . . . the third spindle
from the bottom
missing . . . since God knows when . . .
it was always
kind of dark at the bottom step . . .
the double hung window at the top of the landing
provided light
on a real sunny day you had to squint when you looked up
. . . and you climb the sixteen steps . . .
Sixteen steps up and out of the darkness.

This is not about the beautiful people some of the
various media
have fabricated for us and led us to think they are what
we should all want to be . . .
. . . No . . .
There are no handsome and dashing Harvard professors . . .
No shapely tall sirens with long red hair, green eyes
and very expensive boots.
No millionaires, not always correct . . .
always brilliant . . . always perfections
. . . It's just about people . . .
The guy who looks in the mirror the next morning and says . . .
"I should have . . ."
Mechanics with dirt under their fi ngernails, factory girls,
bartenders, bakers, butchers and street processions.
An old man's recollections of his childhood . . .
Realizing . . . much too late . . . It was a
different time . . . a different place.

St. Paul sort of puts it all into perspective . . .

The First Letter of St. Paul to the Corinthians:

Consider your own calling, brothers and sisters. Not many of you were wise by human standards, not many of you were powerful, not many were of noble birth. Rather, God chose the foolish of the world to shame the wise, and God chose the lowly and despised of the world, those who count for nothing, to reduce to nothing those who are something, so that no human being might boast before God.

Different Time

It was a different time. It was a time of button flies on trousers. It was a time when girls put little crocheted hankies on their head when they entered a church. Women wore hats to Mass on Sunday mornings, some with little black netted veils, full-breasted stout women. Church bells would ring especially on Sunday mornings.

"*Fa subito* (hurry) . . . you'll be late . . . Gotta get to church before the Gospel . . . If not, what's the use of going to Mass? Did you go to Mass?"

"Sure, Ma!"

"What color were the vestments? What was the Gospel about? Who did you go with?"

In those days—what, air-conditioning?—they gave employees salt tablet in July and August in the mills . . . Pa would stuff some scrap pieces of cloth, maybe a nice piece of fleece lining into his lunch pail. Ma would fi nd some use for them. Sometimes Pa would take a piece of the "strap," a piece of belt from the long belts that drove the different machines and pumps in the textile mills' dye department. They were much too short to salvage, just junk, but just the right width to shape and carve out a leather sole for one of the boys' shoes—small tacks, some glue, like new, just like New York.

At Christmastime, we'd have easy-to-peel tangerines. The skins were placed on the hot firebox end of the big black stove. They'd cook, emitting a fresh-orange-scent odor. There'd be chestnuts (*castani*) roasting in the oven on a tin plate. We have to eat them when they're still warm. They don't taste as good when they get cold. They can get gummy and then hard, not good. Cigars—Italian stogies, hard, roughly made Tuscany cigar for the old-timers; White Owls or Dutch Masters, with their smooth outer skin for the American and maybe some older-timer's son; then a little later, cigarettes; Camels and Luckies, all nonfilters (easier to field strip when you were in the army).

. . . They were different times . . .

. . . They were the best of times . . .

Lunch bag—Tony once watched Paulie. After eating his lunch, Paulie straightened out his lunch bag and pressed it flat on the cafeteria table and folded it into a small square and put it into his pocket. Tony's mother often told Tony to save his lunch bag and bring it home so that she could use it again, but Tony felt embarrassed when he did it; it was not hip. The other guys might laugh at him if they saw him do it. Tony didn't laugh at Paulie, not that time anyway.

"Did you bring the bag home?"

"Aw, Ma, I forgot again!"

After a while, Ma won't bother to ask.

. . . And the worst of times . . .

The Feast

We'll Call Him Tony
They All Came Scrambling
Tony is Found
Fridone Hustling . . . Free Bottle
Gnumariedi . . . last glass
Phone Call . . . Chewing Gum
Winding the Clock . . . Funeral

We'll Call Him Tony

We will call him Tony. That is not his real name but it fits both the story and the character. Tony is an old man, and maybe some of the kids would say, "A real old man!" He has plowed through a number of decades and often wonders about his experiences. He's heard somewhere—because he has had very few original thoughts—the question or riddle: "Does someone have 'x' number of years experience or one year experience 'x' number of times?" He pondered.

Yeah, he thought after taking still another sip of that grape, *that Dickens guy was right on the money; he hit the nail on the head.* He held the thought, and it grew, and it impressed him even more with its fundamental simplicity. His lips moved slightly as he softly repeated the words aloud, "They were the best of times and they were the worst of times." "Yeah, right on the money, right in the 'Name of the Father'; in a lousy thirteen words, this guy Charles Dickens says it all. Just thirteen, and *whadda* ya *gunna* say? How ya *gunna* say it anyway? How?"

Today all that Tony has to do is lightly tap the computer key marked Page Up and before him appears documentation of the "best of times and the worst of times." And this can be scrolled up or even down for that matter, all in a blink of an eye.

He has been trying to put down on paper some of his experiences, his feelings, and yes, those memories. Those memories so deeply imbedded in his brain that they will not or cannot ever be forgotten. *Damn it.* he thought. *I wish I could forget some 'dem ones and only 'member the good ones.*

He presses the Page Up button and in his mind, and in his soul (if he or anybody else has or had one) he sees and feels: the brownstone tenements, the cold-water five-room flat, second- and third-floor rear staircases, a coal stove in the dead of winter fed by a Kafka-like coal bucket as black as sin itself. He sees and remembers a time when his flat, especially the kitchen, had its own distinct welcoming smell to it; and it was safe, always safe. Safe just because his mother and father were there—that's why.

It was a world of alleyways: kids playing cowboys and Indians, cops and robbers. It was time of Friday night baths and one towel. It was a world and a time of playing baseball either on the coal cinder covered school yard or at the vacant lot by the Utica-Mohawk Sheet textile mills. On a good day, maybe three baseball gloves, two old baseball bats (both had nails in them to keep them together, one more than the other) and sticky black electrical tape from the knob almost up to the Louisville Slugger label.

It was a world and a time of girls jumping rope on the sidewalk and alleyways, and skipping and hopping through the hopscotch patterns. Somebody always had a piece of white blackboard chalk for school—contributed (voluntarily or involuntarily) by the school system. They used the chalk to draw and number in those tricky (sometimes square and sometimes triangular) patterns on the concrete. With the grace and poise of a Russian ballerina the girls would compete. So what if their hair was up in pigtails and one of their knees has a scab from an earlier fall? It never once—not once—affected their stellar performance.

Tony recalls that Italian was always spoken by his parents and aunts, especially indoors, in the safe confines that constituted *his* home. Outdoors, on the street, with the other kids it was English, but not the best English.

Those immigrants in the old neighborhood dragged a lot of southern Italian and Sicilian baggage with them to *l'America.* The patron saints of their villages were never forgotten and their feast day always remembered and celebrated. The immigrants felt they had a lot to be grateful for, more so if in the depression their father had a job. In their hearts of hearts, especially the women, they all knew the Blessed Mother and their hometown patron saint were responsible for their good fortune—here in the "promised land."

Tony's mother's village venerated St. Michael the Archangel. His father's village venerated the two Lebanese physicians: Saints Cosmo and Damiano. The holy brothers were always referred to as *santi medici* (saintly doctors) by the paisanos.

The size and the intensity of the devotions and celebrations of the feast day were contingent upon the number of paisanos in the parish and in the neighborhood.

Tony could "page down" through the decades. Now it is *His American Dream*—his suburbia home, his two-stall garage, his IRAs, mutual funds, cell phone, telephone, television, same-sex marriages, the Holy Roman Catholic Church being beaten up, and *the Yankees don't win 'em like they used too!*

They are—and were indeed—the best of times and the worst of times. With a little bit of luck, maybe it won't get *worser*—anyway *'snot supposed to!*

They All Came Scrambling

They all came scrambling, pushing and shoving and laughing, running up the rear staircase: Tony's older brothers, Salvatore and Angelo; their cousins Antoinette, Marie Delores, Mary Frances, Anthony, Carmella, Rosie, Frances, and Johnny—all of them, happy kids, with sparkling jet-black eyes like olives; noisy kids, with their youthful and adolescent voices, and all at various pitches; happy kids!

They had been to the feast of Saints Cosmas and Damian most of the afternoon. They pitched pennies, and some of them would concentrate so hard that the tip of their tongues would inadvertently slip out the corner of their mouth. They would pinch that copper penny, aiming (closing one eye for accuracy) at very slippery glass targets—cups and saucers—which were sitting there in the center of the stand. They'd inhale then let it go and hope it would get in there—hoping.

Other pennies went to the betting of the horses. There was a long shiny enamel-painted board with seven different-colored horses' heads beautifully painted, each in their individual block, numbered on the bottom and in the center. The kids would bet a penny on their favorite number, or maybe the color of the horse's mane, or *justa* hunch, *justa* hunch.

The man would say, "No more bets!" Then with one hand, he would reach up and grip the big wheel that had the numbers 1 through 7 on it, very close together; most have been a zillion "1s," a zillion "2s," zillion number "3s," and so on. Zillions! Then the man would quickly check the betting board and the pretty painted horses on it, making sure the pennies were still there. Flicking his wrist, the wheel became alive, exploding—the numbers became a blur—a rapid clickity-clackity staccato, almost one sound. The kids would inhale deeply, holding their breath, watching it, not blinking. The bettors looked at the spinning wheel; the man looked at his board, the money, making sure none of the players had a change of heart. During the course of the day and night, the numbers would come and go; he only had to pay on one—the winner. The remaining bets went into his cigar box—not everyone wins.

The kids would strain to listen; they'd squint their eyes. "Don't blink, you'll miss *sumptin*!" said one while they listened to the cadence of the clicking. It's slowing down ("Come on number two . . . *cum-ona* number two!"). The kids continued watching, hoping, and praying. "I played number two, didn't I?" one says with a glance at the board, eyes darting back and forth, looking for the number. The wheel is slowing. They're all gasping. They again hold their breath as if that would control the wheel.

"*Whaddya* doin'? You ain't *gunna* steer that thing!"

"Oh yes, I can!"

The wheel stops. Somehow, it always seems to stop suddenly. The clicker bounces, leaning toward the opposite direction it is traveling but would never go back to the number it passed. The winner beams; the losers are disappointed. "See? *Whadda* I tell ya?"

From the edge of the brightly painted betting board, the man quickly cupped his right hand, raking up all of the losers' pennies, allowing them to drop heavily into an open cigar box that he held with an iron grip in his left hand. He then would flip the cigar box lid, closing it shut on all those other pennies that more than half filled it—along with the losers' dreams. The lid made a very soft, muffled thud. (The losers heard the thud, their audio senses honed earlier by the clicking of the wheel.)

The man would then ask the winner(s) to identify their coin(s), and with his thumb and index fi nger, he would noisily snap one of his pennies next to it. The winner(s) would scoop it up, and the new painted betting board, with the pretty numbered horses, was once again cleared. The man's honor and reputation remained intact; the winners were paid; the losers had his condolences.

One of the kids (a winner) bought and shared a big bag of salty *lupinos* (yellow soft legumes with a film like shell soaked in brine). He rarely spat out the salty shells but mostly ate both shell and bean. Another would buy and share a string of round hazel nuts and stop to stare at those huge, huge blocks of nougat candy cut by a black-handled pointed knife, the kind you'd see in a horror movie when the villain would be sneaking up on the helpless lady.

Some kids would buy and share a small cone of lemon ice, which was artistically (and very theatrically) applied to the cone with a common kitchen spoon, for three cents; a large cone was a nickel.

"*Wanna* a lick, Johnny?"

"Yeah, you bet . . . *tanks*!"

He had to give him a lick! Johnny gave him three hazel nuts earlier. Fair is fair!

Big men were standing in their stalls, frying sausage and peppers; women from various *società* (*s*) were slicing and then stretching pieces of bread dough, dropping it into a pan of hot oil, quickly turning them over to fry the other side, putting the pizza fritta on a napkin, sprinkling sugar on it. Some of those stout ladies would put an extra pinch on if one asked nicely, or if they knew one's mother or were some *comarra*. There were stands that even sold hot dogs, for God's sake! Real honest to God "Mayor-I-Can" food on what always seemed to be a raw hot dog bun. The bread would always stick to the roof of one's mouth. (What *kinda* bread is this? It ain't got no crust?)

The feast took place in a very special section of East Utica. This magical area's perimeter was Catherine Street to Pelletieri Avenue to Jay Street, to Kossuth Avenue and then back to Catherine Street. The streets were, of course, closed to vehicular traffic during the feast. Multicolored sixty-watt light bulbs of red, white, green, and some places blue were strung across the streets from blue four-by-four fourteen-foot-tall poles. They had been lit since before nine in the morning and would not be turned off until well after midnight.

All that those happy kids wanted, upon bursting into Aunt Chiara's flat, was something to eat (quickly), go to the bathroom (some had a more urgent need than others), and beg for another quarter from one of the adults (chances were always better if they asked from an adult male, who was sitting and talking at the kitchen table, drinking wine and eating some provolone cheese, pepperoni, or black olives and bread). But of paramount importance, to all the kids, was permission to go back out into the streets again.

They wanted out again into the crowded streets because the feasting outside was overwhelming to the senses; the sounds, music and singing and shouting; the aromas, peppers and sausage, frying pizza fritta; the sights, colored lights overhead; the stands, some with bright awnings; the pretty majorettes; colorful uniforms of the band members (including La Banda Rossa est. 1905) with their horns and drums—just the hustle and the bustle, just East Utica. God bless East Utica.

Then Tony's mom quietly asked, "A dove sta Antonio? (Where is Tony?)"

His brothers instantly glanced at one another; their lower jaw dropped and their eyes widened. They turned Antoinette. She was one of the eldest and was given charge of Tony, who was not yet four and a half years old. Antoinette glared back at them because sometime during the afternoon she handed Tony over to them to "watch." She and some of her "older" female cousins wanted to walk around the feast and hoped that boys would flirt with them.

Tony's brothers got into it. "Yea, Big Jerk, you were supposed to watch him!"

"*Whaddya* talkin' 'bout?"

"He was with us when we went to the school yard.

You forgot we had him!" Angelo shouted back.

"So did you!" Salvatore returned the volley.

When his brothers took charge of Tony they decided to go to the Brandegee School yard to watch the drum and bugle corps march and parade around. A drum and bugle spectacular right there on the school grounds. But they really wanted to watch the short skirts and boots and the fleshy thighs of the majorettes and see just how high the hem of their short skirt would come up when they spun around as they twirled their batons. Sometimes, but not too often, their eyes would rise to see if the majorette's hat was going to fall off. All that the majorettes had holding their tall, gold and white cadet hats, was a thin chin strap. But that was then, but now Tony is lost! And Tony is not yet four and a half years old!

Tony's aunts and his mom shouted in unison, in broken English but mostly in Italian. The message was crystal clear: "Go now . . . find him . . . right now . . . and don't one of you come back until you find him! *FA subito! Va-teen!* (Be quick about it! Go now!)"

The kids were not frolicking nor laughing when they stampeded—nearly all tumbling—down the rear staircase. They poured out into the alleyway and then out on Catherine Street. This was serious—feast or no feast! The girls would turn right toward Pelletieri and the boys would turn left toward Kossuth. The plan was to go around the block. The girls turned right off Catherine on to Pelletieri and right again on to Jay Street. The boys turned left off Catherine on to Kossuth and left again on to Jay Street. They would meet in the middle of the block by Patsy's Chicken store on Jay Street. If one of the search parties found Tony, the eldest would take him home immediately, the remainder of the group would advise the other group.

On the northeast corner of Kossuth and Jay streets was a two-story white-frame structure with a barbershop on the ground floor. The shop occupied half of the structure's ground floor; the remaining space was a small apartment.

The second floor was one large apartment. The second floor apartment staircase opened on to Jay Street, the first-floor apartment front door opened on to Kossuth. The barbershop had two large plate-glass windows: one facing Kossuth; the other, Jay. Each had identical signs (in script) painted on them: Joe's Barbershop, in white with a thin line of black shadowing around the edges of the words. Joe had a four-foot red, white, and blue barber pole outside attached to the building by the front door. Inside he had two potted fig trees by each of the plate-glass windows. His shop had three barber chairs: white porcelain and black cushions. To this day, the guys from the old neighborhood still call it "Joe the Barber's corner." Diagonally located from Joe's barbershop (on the southwest side) was a very large and impressive three-story brownstone with commercial /tenant occupancy. The first floor was totally commercial; the remaining two stories housed six flats. Way up (above the third-story flats and slightly below the roof line) was the name Perretta neatly formed in block lettering on a gray concrete slab. It was a bank when Tony's father came to America; but since then, it has housed a food distributor, a grocery store, a bakery, a coffee shop, a taproom, then a VFW, and so it went. But it was always big, always impressive to look at; it was solid, broad-shouldered and strong like a fortress. Especially if one was young and sitting on the street curb, catching glimpses of the building through the milling crowd.

During the feast, right at Joe the Barber's corner (literally at the corner's curving curb and the on-the-street—and not the barbershop's—sidewalk) one could buy roasted chickpeas. A big, big man (not only by the standards of a four-and-half-year-old but by all the kids) sold them in little white paper bags. The big man was rounded, even more rounded than Patsy the Chicken Man, more rounded than Uncle Joe.

He and his operation was a marvel to behold, a wonder to see, to hear, and to smell and taste. The chickpeas were roasted in the biggest metal bowl Tony had ever seen. He could sit in it. The kettle had a rounded bottom and sat on a specially made iron tripod stand. The stand was designed to accommodate the inverted dome of the kettle and also allow for the fire underneath. Wood and charcoal were used as fuel, and it would get hot if one stood too close.

The big man half filled the brass kettle with white sand. When the sand got warm, he added four or five big scoops of little white chickpeas. He'd stir it occasionally, using what looked to Tony to be half of a wooden oar. His wife sat nearby on a four-legged stool by the hundred pound bags of chickpeas. She had a closed Dutch Master's cigar box on her lap. By her left leg was a brown paper grocery bag that contained an ample supply of smaller white paper bags. During the course of the evening, and as needed, she'd reach in there, pick one out, and give it to her husband. It would be filled with warm chickpeas. The cigar box, which never ever left her lap, was their cashbox.

The big old man would perspire profusely as he worked. He wore a red knotted bandana around his thick neck. It served to absorb the sweat especially from around the nape of the neck. He also used a blue bandana, which was normally tucked into his left rear trouser pocket, or at least two-fifths of it; the remainder hung out of the trouser pocket. It would occasionally swing like a misplaced tail. This one was used to mop his face while he held the stirring paddle with his other hand. (You see, stirring was a two-handed job.)

His chest and upper body was clothed in what appeared to be the top half of a "union suit" (one piece underwear with long sleeves). The first three buttons were undone in an attempt to improve circulation and ventilation to and around his massive chest. He also wore black suspenders that looked like two roads going over and then down the big hill of his stomach and hooking up to his gray trousers' beltline. The suspenders met the trousers at points approximately above his crotch and below his navel; it was difficult to tell exactly. Of the seven buttons of his fly, only four were properly secured. The dark blue golf-type cap (fl at with a brim) was never removed, not even when he wiped the sweat from his face with the blue handkerchief. Tony's Uncle Mike and Uncle Joe wore caps like that; his father used to wear a felt Adams hat.

As the big man stirred the mixture of sand and chickpeas he would sing (?), chant (?), intone (?) something that sounded Italian, but really wasn't—not to Tony anyway! His dialect was not what Tony was used to, although he did recognize a word here or there. A four-and-a-half-year-old boy became mesmerized, sitting on a street curb, looking upward into a living spectacle of life from another world. Who wouldn't?

A customer would come up to the kettle. The big old man would lean his stirring paddle against the kettle, reach for a long-handled perforated ladle, scoop down into the sand and chickpea mixture and then shake the sand back into the kettle. His wife would hand him one of those white paper bags, and the big man would carefully put the contents of the ladle into the bag. He'd have to repeat the process two or three times to get the white bag filled. The customer would step over to where his wife was sitting to pay. His wife, whose hand was all ready, palm up and extended to the customer even before the customer felt the warmth of the chickpeas in his own hand, took the coin. She nodded her thanks and lifted the lid on the cigar box, and the coin would clink as it fell to the bottom of the box. The box would never ever move even a little bit from her lap.

The big old man would then pick up his paddle, start to stir, and sing again. He was like a "Pied Piper" drawing young and old to the chickpea kettle. His wife, dutifully sitting there by their copper kettle, her hands resting on the cigar box, was the caretaker and guardian of the family's financial future.

It must have been a lifetime later—if not more—when Tony and his wife were visiting/touring Greek ruins in Sicily. At one particular site, and upon completion of the tour, the group was given a half hour to visit the various souvenir and food stands that surrounded the scores of buses in the parking area. He and his wife walked by a small umbrella-covered stand when Tony stopped suddenly, pointed, and said to his wife, "Look! Chickpeas! Haven't had them in years; I'm gunna get a bag."

And he promptly did so. In his best Italian, he told the vendor that when he was a kid he would buy chickpeas at various feasts and then proceeded to tell him that they would be warm because the chickpeas were stirred in heated sand. The vendor (to Tony's delight) smiled knowingly and said, "E pui miglia con la sabbia del mar (It is best when you use sand from the sea)." They smiled at each other broadly, and Tony told him to keep the change.

As they walked away, his wife, (who noted the size of the tip) inquired why this surge of generosity on his part. He replied, "Because . . ." but went no further. She asked again. He replied, "Nuttin' . . . 'Snot important . . . wanna try one these?"

It was starting to get dark. The kids, the girl search party and the boy search party, had already met four times in the middle of Jay Street, near Patsy the Chicken Store's alleyway. Nobody saw little Tony, and it was getting dark. If they saw somebody or anyone they knew, the kids would hopefully and excitedly ask, "Did *ya* see Little Tony?"

"*Naw*, I didn't see him. Is he alright?" (Or "No, *whaddsa madder*? Is he lost?") The answers would leave them crestfallen and disappointed, and it would deepen and darken their rapidly growing worst fears: "What if he wandered into an alleyway—and rested and fell asleep and a stray cat or a mad dog or the worst, rats started to eat him? We gotta find him! It's already starting to get dark . . . He is only four and half years old . . . And he is all alone. All alone!"

They decided to reverse the search patterns: the girls making left turns, the boys making right turns. "We gotta find him." The adult men (Tony's uncles) who had come to visit Tony's parents started to fidget and stir uncomfortably and would keep looking up at that yellow-painted clock on a shelf between the two kitchen windows. It wasn't really necessary to study or look at the clock because it sounded every quarter hour and counted out the time at the top of the hour. Earlier, maybe an hour or so, Tony's father excused himself and went out to aid in the search. The conversation among the adult males decreased drastically; they'd sip from their glasses of wine and hope that someone would pick up the conversation. The yellow clock, with a small statuette of a cowboy twirling a lariat directly in the center of the clock and the horse centered above the roman numeral XII, loudly sounded still another hour—six solid bongs. It was getting dark, and the boy was only four and a half years old. As if the six bongs were a secret signal, they all left their wine glasses, some partially filled; left the pepperoni and bread; the black olives and bread; the provolone and bread; and asked for their hats. They had to do something! A boy was missing.

The men left the flat and the women initially busied themselves by putting the food in the icebox. They put the cheese directly on top of a block of ice to have it firm up again, and the olives and pepperoni went in the lower compartment; the bread, in a bag that went outside and on top of the ice box. Before they all sat at the brown metal top table that rested on wooden legs, which also housed a small utensil drawer, they took off their aprons. They put their little black leather imitation pinch purses into their dress pocket, neatly folded the aprons, and laid them on the recently wiped clean tabletop. They sat and interlaced their fingers and placed their hands on the apron. The folded aprons acted as a soft cushion for their hands.

"As soon as Mike comes back, we gotta go; he has gotta go to work at the bakery at two o'clock." And another aunt said more for conversation than advising, *"Si . . . anche Serafino a lovaro domoni al le sei."* The little act of taking off the aprons and folding them, helped calm them—not much—but a little bit. Furthermore, it would save time when the search was over, and the families returned home. The boy had to be found.

Like the men did a bit earlier, they too hoped for some conversation and kept peeking up at the yellow clock with the cowboy twirling a lasso. When the clock would strike a quarter hour or something, one of them inevitably and unintentionally would cluck; and they'd all seem to sink deeper into that quiet quagmire of this unbearable depression. The kitchen became very quiet. They could hear the yellow clock ticking, ticking loudly; it could have been thunder.

Four women, all mothers, in their worried thoughts, and none giving audible sound to those thoughts, were unified in their fervent wishes for the boy's safe and prompt return. Should one have had the power to hear their unspoken words at that moment, it would be the same for all four of them: *"Ave, o Maria, piena de grazia; il Signore è con te . . . "* On the immediate right of the copper kettle (and the old lady clutching a cigar box) at the curb, was a city sewer. The thick (maybe two inches) heavy manhole cover/grate was at least two feet in diameter; the grate grid opening was big enough to let all the running water through, but would prevent a baseball from dropping into that dark circular abyss. It laid flat, level with street tarmac.

That was just the manhole cover. Where the manhole cover met the curb, there was a vertical opening two feet wide and four inches high—all part of the street sewer. This large vertical storm opening was encased in cast iron and not protected by a grate or a screen. With many a baseball, sometimes even a "rare" tennis ball (that was mostly battered against the high wall by the BOYS entrance at Brandegee and used in handball games), the winner could play as long as he kept winning unless, of course, the kid who owned the ball wanted it back or had to go home. Even black electrical tape-wrapped baseballs—those rare tennis balls—would find their watery demise and eternal doom by skipping over the protective grate of the manhole cover and plunging into that circular, brick-lined sewer hole to disappear forever beneath the dark inky water forever and ever.

For some strange, unknown reason, the tennis balls didn't seem to float (You would think they would, wouldn't you?); but they too seemed to sink like a rock or as fast as any black electrical taped-wrapped baseball would sink. ("Do *ya dink da* tennis balls got so dirty . . . *dat* maybe they did float . . . but maybe we *kan't see 'em 'coss* the water at the bottom of the sewer was so black?") To the left of the sewer manhole and its carnivorous, ball-eating storm opening was probably one of the most attractive, if not the busiest, vending stalls at the feast. It had a red, white and green awning over its entire length. It was a platform made of three four-by-eight sheets of plywood horizontally attached and supported by several wooden carpenter horses, which, like the awning above, was properly skirted by matching colors of the awnings. The stand was a crammed Cornucopia of sort: stringed hazel nuts, toy popguns that had a tiny cork that fit into the barrel of the gun with a string attached (one end on the cork, the other on the rifle/gun). Those huge blocks of nougat candy and the sinister-looking knife that cut it; toys like the red-handled dagger that had a flimsy blade that would disappear back into the scabbard when used to stab someone; and colorful but poorly made walking canes and small silk kerchiefs/scarves for girls were also sold.

The stand was manned by a man and his wife (who patrolled the front), and their daughter and two sons tended the rear—and always at their parents' beckoning call.

Here, on that sewer grate with its storm opening unit (with one of his shoes untied, the other hopelessly knotted) stood and eventually sat young Tony. A very good seat. With the slightest movement of his head, toward nine o'clock on a face of a watch, Tony could look up and watch and admire and smile at the singing big old man stirring the chickpeas. With another slight downward jerk of his head, he could easily watch the lady with the cigar box on her lap, and, if he swung his head to three o'clock and slightly upward, there was the colorful awning, the stacks of merchandise packed on the long stall table. (The phony daggers were the closest to him and his strategically placed position on the sewer—his sewer lookout station.)

The big old man was really the show. Young Tony was fascinated. His voice (something like Italian), the smell of the charcoal and wood burning under the kettle, the sand being sifted out of the perforated ladle, the chickpeas sliding into that little white bag—all that and everything else: the cigar box; the red, white, and green awning; the red-handled daggers, an old lady's outstretched hand, palm up; the wooden paddle being stuck back into the copper kettle, can put a boy into another world. Invisible! Invisible to himself. Invisible to all those around him. No pedestrian traffic crossed over at the sewer; the sounds around him were not his, nor did they belong to anyone else.

And when Tony would face twelve o'clock, tip his head back, the entire panorama (right to left, left to right) would become a three-story brownstone structure that filled the sky and had the name Perretta very near the top. How solid, how much like a kingdom fortress, how big and wide, how strong it looked to a boy only four and a half years old. He and his mother and his father and his two older brothers also lived in a three-story brownstone, with a cantina filled with a lot of quarts of tomatoes, a few quarts of plums and peaches, a dusty/dirty coal bin, and two fifty-five-gallon barrels of wine.

His brownstone had a warm bed that he shared with his middle brother. (His eldest brother slept on a "daybed"—an old army cot—but in the same room.). The bedroom door had two hook/hangers screwed into the rear face of the door. He could not, of course, reach the hook and always had to ask for help to hang clothing. Clothing was never left on the floor, maybe on the doorknob or on a bed, but only as a last resort. The hanger hooks were the only "closets" they had in that room.

It was getting dark and the lights and the sounds and the smells made it easy for a young boy to compare his three-story brownstone with that one, which was now to his immediate front. If he were to sit on the curb directly across from 912 Catherine Street, tip his head back and look at his "home," wouldn't it be like the Perretta building filling the entire sky, being up there in the heavens, and close to god? It's solid—made of reddish brick, not swaying like an old telephone/clothes line pole, just solid.

Justified or not, there was poor Antoinette on the verge of tears, blaming herself for all this trouble and sorrow, thinking, *Why? Why, God, did I give him to his brothers? How stupid of me!* Tony's mother and Miss Bailey and the other teachers at school and all the kids in the class (especially when it came to math) were watching her standing before the blackboard, unable to figure out the problem. The classmates were thinking, *How dumb she is.* They would never say it aloud, but Antoinette knew

they were thinking of it in their thoughts; she could see
it in their faces, in their smirks.

How stupid I am! She kept thinking to herself.

It shamed her and she would secretly wish she was
jumping/skipping rope instead of standing there, confused
and scared, in front of the blackboard with that dusty
piece of chalk in her trembling hand.

*But I must be stupid! Look at all the trouble I caused! Oh
God, please help me find Tony . . . PLEASE . . . I won't be
stupid anymore . . . I'll try real hard. Please!*

She was a skinny awkwardly tall girl crying in the
wilderness for divine intervention. A girl with a pleasant
smile and sparkling eyes was the best skip rope jumper
on the block, but failed the third grade twice, fifth grade
once, and finally passed the sixth grade with the dreaded
stigma of "promotion in danger." All the *Merikan* teachers
at Brandegee, Mrs. Urter, Miss Wilson, Mrs. Baker, Miss
Bailey, knew her ilk; she, poor Antoinette, would stay in
the system, probably never reach the eighth grade, drop
out on her sixteen birthday (if not sooner), and end up
in one of the textile mills.

Just another factory girl.

"I won't be stupid anymore, god, honest . . . I'll try
very, very hard . . . only please . . . please let me find little
Tony . . . Please . . ."

(And stupid is just a word, a simple six-letter word; but
does it mean the same to you as it does to me? or him? or
them? How about god . . . ? What does it mean to him?
Anyway, God did not have to make her any smarter,
because she was never stupid.)

Antoinette and three of her female cousins found
themselves again at Joe the Barber's corner. It must have

been the tenth time they were there crossing the crowded intersection. The girls' heads swinging back and forth, searching and searching, still asking acquaintances and friends if they had seen Tony.

Then, just then, as if all the saints and the angels and the archangels and God (himself) up there in heaven finally heard this never-ending petition for help and divine guidance from that part of East Utica, Antoinette's eyes swung from that old lady sitting, holding a closed Dutch Master cigar box and that brightly lit awning-covered stand/stall, and dropped—oh!—so slightly.

A little boy was sitting on the sewer storm drain. The boy had been there and had been invisible all that afternoon. Well into dusk and darkness of the evening unafraid and just watching.

Antoinette, the best skip rope jumper on the block and soon (within three and a half years) to be "just another textile factory worker," gasped; her heart must have stopped; the gasp forced air into her lungs. She had to pinch her sphincter. Even with that, she involuntarily discharged a teaspoon of urine; she tried to scream but could not; and then, out loud she shouted, "I've found him . . . I've found him!"

Tony suddenly felt himself being pulled and quickly lifted off his storm sewer perch; in an instantaneous second, his little body was being twisted. He saw Antoinette's face; then his cheek was against her cheek, and his nose was in her ear and by her hair. He could feel the wetness on her cheek from her tears and somehow soon tasted the saltiness of them. He wondered what was happening, what was wrong. Antoinette clutched him with one arm around his lower back and rump, the other hand and arm pressing his neck to her face, no longer shouting but just whispering, "I've found him . . . I've found him . . . Oh, thank you, sweet Jesus . . . thank you, sweet Jesus . . . thank you, Mother of God." She was crying, and she was running through the crowded street. She was squeezing the boy as if she would never let him go again.

But she would. Soon, as fast as those skip rope-jumping legs could carry her, she would deliver her precious human cargo to someone who (if possible) loved Tony more than her—her favorite aunt, whose eyes always looked so sad to her. The jostle and the squeezing and the bouncing of the race home was causing Tony's untied shoe to start to loosen its already-weak grip on his foot. He tried to twist his ankle sideways and his toes upward to keep the shoe attached. Down the alley they flew, up the four concrete steps of the rear entrance stoop (his shoe finally fell and landed on the second step of the stoop), passed the gray alleyway door. Antoinette released her death-grip hold from the back of Tony's neck (he had long since put both of his arms around her neck and holding on for dear life) and with her now-free hand, she reached and found the staircase railing. She started pulling and climbing those sixteen wooden steps. On the second step, she stopped, whispering her thanks to Jesus and the Mother of God, and started yelling, "I got 'em . . . I've found him . . . I got 'em . . . He is all right . . . He is all right . . . I got him . . . He was at Joe the Barber's corner . . . He is okay."

In that long, narrow kitchen, four women, all mothers, heard the news and gasped; two broke out in tears. Tony's Zia Lucia was up and like a shot ran and opened the yellow screen door, all the time repeating, "*Grazia a Dio . . .*

Grazia a Dio." She, who had nine of her own children at the time, with three more to eventually come, held the screen door wide open with her left hand and stepped as far back into the hallway as she could to allow easier access for her running niece and her cargo. With her right hand, Zia Lucia made all of her fingers touch her thumb, kissed them, and reached out and touched the boy's face as he was carried past. She kissed all her fingers again and was just able to touch Antoinette's back as she continued into the kitchen.

Antoinette offered Little Tony to his mother.

When Tony's ma heard Antoinette coming up the stairs, announcing and heralding the good news, she immediately rose like the other mothers in the room and said, "*Grazia a Dio!*" As she saw them burst into the kitchen, her knees got very, very weak and wobbly, and she had to sit down. Antoinette bent down slightly when she got in front of Tony's mother, and his feet were finally touching the linoleum-covered floor on "solid" ground. Tony automatically, and as if on cue, half turned and hugged his mother's neck. His once very worried mother was inhaling deeply in short quick bursts. Her nostrils flaring, she clenched her teeth ever so tightly as if to suppress any sobs that might escape from deep inside her and squeezed her eyelids to keep the tears inside. Inside where they belonged, but it didn't work; the tears flowed. She hugged him tightly, and little Tony tasted salt again.

He still didn't know what was happening.

Zia Grazia, Antoinette's mother, was the first to gently take Tony from his mother's weakened arms. She lifted him up and pulled him into her enormous breasts and rocked him slowly and kissed him. Then his other Zia Grazia la Coppuco, Uncle Mike's American-born wife, hugged, squeezed him, and kissed him too. Zia Lucia got her real kisses and hugs. Everybody was crying except Tony. Antoinette, willingly or unwillingly, was forced to follow Tony in the same pattern, hugging, crying, and kissing. "Grazia a Dio! Grazia a Dio!"

Aunt Lucy was the one who eventually gave Tony back to his mother, who was still seated, still weak-kneed and crying, the ocean of tears slightly diminishing. She took her youngest, placed her cheek on his, and rocked back and forth slightly. She savored the moment she waited all these hours for and feared may never come. The three mothers/aunts all asking the virgin, all of them talking at once, asking the same questions in different ways, interpreting the response in different ways, rephrasing the questions, reinterpreting the same response.

The tenement flat was now very happy and very alive and very loud with the excitement that only stout Mediterranean mothers and their young daughters can generate. The yellow clock (which kind of looked like a miniature of the Utica Public Library on Genesee Street, only with a big circular white face and roman numerals in the center) sat there upon its high shelf above the kitchen table and between those two tall windows. The ticking of the clock, the bong of the quarter hours, the count of the hour, which one time dominated and shattered the silence of these worried women, was now not heard; and the bongs, not important. Like a boy whose mother was gently rocking him in her arms, he tried to whisper into her ear, "*Mamma, hai perdutto na scarpa* (Ma, I lost a shoe)"; but it was not heard and not important.

Tony Is Found

At about the middle of the block on Jay Street, the news was starting to spread very quickly. Many of those who didn't know Tony or what had happened, and who might have only seen and heard someone running and dodging through the crowd (creating a minor commotion in the already-noisy and festive atmosphere—a ripple) allowed the messenger; hence the message to pass. The messenger passed, and the messenger passed and not heard the message—not important.

The messenger, one of the cousins, was racing through the crowd, looking for family members and friends. When spotted, he'd hardly stopped just slackened his forward motion a bit and bouncing and hopping on one foot, joyfully announcing the news.

"We've found him! We've found him! Antoinette found him . . . He's okay . . . He's all right . . ."

The recipients of the heralded good news would immediately fire questions at the messenger who was already starting to accelerate down the block. His reply came over his shoulder. "By Joe the Barber's corner . . . Antoinette found him sitting on a . . ." The street noise absorbed the rest of the fading report.

The cousins, especially those who were members of the original search parties that went out so long ago, looked at one another and asked one another the same question, some repeating what they just heard, "By Joe the Barber's corner? . . . Can that be? . . . Weren't we just *dare* . . . weren't we *dare* a million times today *lookin' for 'em*? We looked all over a million times . . . a million times . . .

you and me . . . all over . . . Where could he have been? *Whadda* he say, 'Antoinette found him sitting'? Sitting on what? . . . *Did ya* hear what he said, sitting on what?" None of them could answer nor explain, just yet.

The vernacular was a world of *dah* and *dose* and *dem* and *dese* and *nuttin'* or *sumptin';* for some, those pronunciations would never totally disappear, often inadvertently slipping into daily usage.

The King's English was always mutilated and shamefully abused by those Brandegee kids, especially at that age. Drop an *s* here, put it *dare;* change a tense, create a stronger word, like *worser* and stuff like that. So if someone from Buckingham Place happened to be standing on Jay Street that particular evening, he or she would have distinctly heard one of Tony's cousins say, "It *snot* important!"

For the first time in that long afternoon and early dusk, the kids were happy again. And it felt good, *sooo* good! Little Tony was home and safe; the family was together; the stars up there (above the many strands of red and green, and sometimes blue feast lights strung out over Jay and Catherine and Kossuth and Pelletieri) were starting to twinkle, safe and sure in their eternal positions in the heavens; and God is in his heaven. How did the kids know that for sure? Dummy—how could anyone have found four-and-a-half-year-old Tony without his help?

The news bearer kept running and dodging through the crowded street less than a half block left on Jay, then at the short block of Pellettieri turned by John Blaze's building on to Catherine and just went to the middle of the block—he's done! Maybe? *Naw!* He decided he would ru it again, only this time in reverse, back to Pellettieri over Jay to Kossuth. He had to make sure he didn't miss anybody. It's not a small thing; this was important, and all of the family *gotta* know—Tony is safe. The rerun turned out to be financially beneficial to our panting messenger. The boy spotted Zio Donato and Zio Serafi no (Uncle Dan and Uncle Sam) near the middle of the block on Pellettieri. He ran up between them, stopped, pulled off his hat, and like the sergeant (?) from his green *Prose and Poetry* book story (seventh grade reading) "Message to Garcia," reported loud and accurately. And for the same reason he took off his hat (respect), he relayed the report in Italian. Uncle Dan beamed; it was his daughter Antoinette; Uncle Sam tipped his head back and laughed, repeating, "Brava a Donetta! Brava Donetta! Brava . . . Brava!" Uncle Dan reached into his pocket and gave the runner a quarter. Uncles and nephew, all were smiling from ear to ear. The boy said thank you in two languages and in the same breath. He replaced his hat and sped off to complete his mission, to his "Garcia!" (He was not only happier, if that were possible; but in his mind and his world, much richer.)

As the runner was reporting to the instantly relieved uncles, three couples (a Calabrese and his wife, his wife's sister, who had just married a man from Bari, and another Calabrese couple who was not only from the same village, but from the same street) passed by. The three men walked a pace and a half in front of the women. The women were clutching their black imitation leather Sunday purses, and their purses were hidden and/or camouflaged by their black shawls. The men, with their suit jackets just draped over their shoulders, hands locked behind and at the small of their backs, heard the cousin telling the uncles. The women also heard. They all moved slowly with the flow, awed by the sights and sounds; not a word was said—not out loud anyway.

The men, in their silence, thought and felt down deep in their souls, "This is good . . . a boy . . . lost . . . a boy found . . . a boy safe . . . a happy family." The three Calabrese women believed the news to be a good omen not only for the once-lost boy and his family, but for themselves. It was a blessed thing to hear good news and even more blessed when it came on a Saint's day and feast. The saints will not only lift any *mal-occhi* (evil eye) from the boy, but also his family and (*Grazia a Dio*) even us! They smiled inwardly and were happy for the boy's mother and themselves. And God, along with the saints whose day was being celebrated, could easily hear the women's unspoken words: *"Ave o Maria . . . piena de grazia; il Signore e con te . . ."*

They continued to move slowly with the flow, taking in the sights, no one speaking.

It was Uncle Serafino who first saw his two brother-in-laws standing by the sausage stand; their heads swung from left to right, right to left. He nudged Uncle Dan and with his chin pointed them out; they both knew, just by looking and seeing the way Pietro and Mike acted, that General Garcia's sergeant never got the word to them. They walked up to them boldly and told them. Tony's father did a very uncharacteristic thing, uncharacteristic for him anyway: he embraced Uncle Dan, and Uncle Dan—heard but never once told another living soul that Peter the Rock, Peter the strongest one—stifled and choked down a sob from deep down in his chest. They patted Uncle Dan on the back, like it was he who found Tony and not his tall and skinny Antoinette.

Antoinette, whose only claim to any fame—if any at all—was that she was the best skip rope jumper on Catherine Street, yet would someday end up in the textile mills, just like all the other grade school dropouts, suddenly seemed special; but not this special tonight.

Uncle Mike, Uncle Dan, Uncle Sam, and Tony's father were all openly relieved; and it showed in their eyes which quickly became kind of watery, although nobody would ever in a thousand years get one of them to admit it was tears.

Uncle Serafino, the eldest and one of the wiser ones, suggested going to Goomba Joe's Restaurant and having a beer. "Let the ladies cry themselves out for a bit, 'The boy is safe!'"

Inside the barroom, it was only Serafino and Michael who were able to find elbow space (literally and figuratively) at the bar. They stood facing one another at the bar, almost belt buckle to belt buckle, and certainly toe-to-toe. Elbows pressing against their stomach and chest, tipping their heads back and bending a little backward, they'd sip the cold beer. They would carefully pass Peter and Dan full glasses of beer. This feast was (and would remain so for many, many years to come) Goomba Joe Lucarelli's biggest weekend of the year—and not only at the bar.

In Tony's neighborhood, there was an abundance of *piasani*, it seemed like almost all of them had come from or lived nearby, Alberobello, Cisternino, Logorotundo, Monopoli, Martino Franca: beautiful-sounding words that one could more easily sing than pronounce. This

feast day in late September was to honor patron saints of
one of these musical-sounding village names. It came to be
by word of mouth or correspondence or announcement
from pulpits of Italian parishes throughout the county
and beyond or a *commara* told another *commara*.
Whatever, come the weekend of the feast, they came.
They would come in overcrowded automobiles, the
youngest squirming on adult laps. They would come
in church-sponsored buses. They'd come early in the
morning and leave late at night; piasano or almost
piasano or a relative of piasano—Italians. Tony's mother
and aunts always referred to all of them as *le forestieri*.
They were referred to as foreigners, not because they
were not Italian or a true piasano from the same village
in the old country, but because they were foreigners to
the neighborhood.

The Sicilians or the Romanos or the Calabrese or even
the Poles, who lived on Nichols Street; or the blacks, who
lived on Hubbel and Jay Street; the Jew, Mr. Block, who
had a dry goods store in the 900 block of Bleecker—all of
them who lived or worked in the neighborhood, none of
them were foreigners. Most forestieri were good people,
people that you were required to respect. It was devotion
to the saints that brought them to the neighborhood. The
streets were always crowded. In Goomba Joe's Restaurant
men would stand two, three deep at the bar. The long
mahogany bar had an equally long footrest railing rising
six inches off the often beer-splashed and certainly beer-
smelling wooden floor. Over the years, the top of the metal
pipe footrest had long since been shined (almost looking
like polished silver) by the shoe soles and heels of working

men's boots and shoes; but it never complained, either by sagging or weakening or wobbling under that weight of thousands of tired feet. The long foot-polished crossbar of the bar rail was supported by short five-and-half-inch (every three feet) posts that were anchored firmly to the floor and rail.

On the floor, and centered directly beneath the footrest rail, were four strategically placed spittoons. These spittoons were nothing like what the kids saw in western movies—those shiny brass ones with a funnel-like opening top, a smaller neck below opening into a globelike bottom. No. Nothing like that. These spittoons were of white porcelain, with a half-inch blue stripe painted around the circumference. The spittoons resemble a twelve-by-four-inch (diameter and height) cake pan. They had a lid (with its blue ring around the circumference), and the lid had a three-inch hole in the center. The lid was designed to slope downward to its center. In spite of the size of the lid and its blue-striped outer rim and (from a standing position), the black three-inch-hole target in the center, some customers still missed it.

Directly beneath the hustle and bustle of the crowded bar, below that long mahogany bar and below the shiny (on the top anyway) bar rail, and below the four spittoons and below the damp and beer-smelling wooden floor was a basement. The basement was called Goomba Joe's private gold mine.

Other than storing the numerous wooden kegs of beer, supplies, and other stuff, it housed a brick oven—not a pizza oven, much better; furthermore, Goomba Joe did not make pizzas; that was for bakeries, not restaurants.

(Who wants or needs all that flour, flour dust, pizza dough, or pizza boxes in a busy kitchen?)

Joe's oven was stoked up and used every Saturday night (Fridays and Sundays during the feast) for preparing meats that were so sweet, rustic, and succulent that it would cause a person to salivate and overwhelm his natural sense of taste and smell. (After six long decades, some still vividly remember the rich taste, the oral sensation, the juice of the meat, and the tickling of the taste buds aided by a flush of saliva. The mere thought of it satisfied a much-different hunger.)

Sausage and lamb, if you wanted, but it was the gnumariedi; that's what the piasano and le forestieri really wanted. They'd order them by the "spit" and eat like they've never eaten before and then in the months to come would savor and relive the experience. Gnumariedi. Just liver (sometimes another "soft" meat) and basil and bay leaves and other herbs wrapped altogether and then placed in a pork intestine/casing. Down in Joe's gold mine it became hot and crowded and hectic. On a "normal" Saturday night, two good men could handle the demand and activity but not during the feast. There was a trap door just off to the right of the bar that gave you access into the basement. The door, which was "hooked" open during the heavy action, opened on to a wooden staircase that descended into the "mine"; there was no handrail. The runners, with bundles or full platters, would be scrambling up the rickety staircase all day long from noon till midnight. The trip back down, they'd be carrying slips of papers containing orders for the next platter or bundle and sometimes a schooner of cold beer for the guys working *lo forno* (the oven), a.k.a. *the miners*.

Fridone and Finnocchio were working in the mine this weekend. Being bachelors, and living at a nearby boarding house, they were normally just regular patrons at Joe's. They were fixtures. The smaller Fridone emerged from the mine, carrying two plates of gnumariedi; and as he danced and maneuvered past Dominic and Bull Dog who were tending bar, he spotted Tony's father and his uncles and nodded a quick hello. He hurriedly continued his mission, which was to put the filled plates on a designated table at the far end of the bar. Within seconds, one of the dining room waiters would suddenly appear, check the order slip, scoop up the plates, and hurry off.

The waiters would do quicksteps down a short hallway (the women's room on the right) and would disappear into a very crowded and noisy main dining room. The main dining room door faced Pelletieri Avenue. Painted on the glass panel of the door was "Ladies Entrance"

On this weekend only, women were allowed with their husbands and children to sit at one of the nine tables in the barroom. The women (and the children when and if possible) never sat facing the bar.

Fridone Hustling . . . Free Bottle of Wine

On the way back (using the server's side of the bar), Fridone paused momentarily and in a sort of shout, because of the constant din at the bar, asked Tony's father if they found Little Tony. Peter beamed, and rather than shouting back from his too-deep-back position at the bar, only nodded vigorously in response. Good old Fridone, who loved to tease Young Tony over the years and who was earlier advised of his disappearance, smiled broadly. No smile of relief was ever broader. "Ayaa! Ayaa!" was all he said and made that long reach across the bar to shake Peter's hand.

Tony's uncle, Mike, the bold and brassy uncle who had been in America since 1913, reached over and grasped Fridone's wrist. He pulled him closer to him, stretching a bit over the bar, and whispered (or tried to) into Fridone's ear. The little man seemed to understand and nodded vigorously. He pulled away, but then Uncle Mike pulled him back and spoke into his right ear again. Poor old Fridone nodded just as vigorously as before, but this time he smiled broadly. He then sidestepped Bull Dog, had to drop and lean his shoulder a bit into Dominic's apron bib to move past him. In four steps, he reached the creaky wooden steps, the mine shaft. He moved on, disappearing into the depth of Joe's gold mine. But not for long.

Down in the mine, it was as hectic as ever. Four men were permanently down there and three runners always going up or coming down. There was a delicious aroma of meat roasting down there in the mine. However, during the course of the long day, the sweet, rich, enticing aroma of meat roasting (which would in most cases cause hungry men to salivate) was no longer noticeable for those seven men. They no longer wished or craved or wanted to *mangiare* (eat)—ahh!—but the same could not be said for their thirst.

The men were stoking the fire with wood and charcoal, laying meat-laden spits over the embers/flames, watching and turning the spits, rewarding themselves occasionally with half a sip of beer, almost becoming mesmerized by the embers of the small inferno, watching the fat dropping from the speared meats and exploding in a crackle even before making contact with the embers.

When the meat was cooked, the spit was lifted from the oven (Joe's gold mine) and placed on a nearby table. At the farthest corner stood two pitchers of cold beer for the "miners". The outer side of the glass beer pitchers immediately became and remained sweaty. It got hot down there.

Another miner, with only one glove (left hand), would pick up the hot meat-loaded spit by the just-as-hot metal handle, and with the dexterity, grace, and agility that only time and sweat and practice can give, he would lift the spit high and point the sword end downward into a large ceramic pasta bowl. Then like a bullfighter at the moment of truth, with the back end of a meat cleaver and with a firm downward stroke, he would strip the spit of its contents. He then would turn slightly, toss the barren spit into the cut-down half of a metal drum. The drum was filled with water at the correct depth to cool the hot spits and enable the T end of the spit to hook on to the rim. Sometimes the hiss could be heard when the spits entered the water.

Two spits of gnumariedi to the pasta bowl. With his gloveless right hand, he'd pick up a large salt shaker and sprinkle a generous amount onto the gnumariedi. He then would put down his salt shaker, and with two hands on the rim of the large pasta bowl, he would toss its contents. Sometimes the herb-flavored casing-wrapped liver would go as high as eight inches off the bottom of the bowl. The salt was evenly distributed, which was a good thing, because during the feast Joe and his brother Dominic would remove the salt and pepper shakers from the tables upstairs. For those who wanted more salt, they'd have to ask a busy waiter and hope that he'd remember. With the gnumariedi or the sausage or the lamb properly bowled, he would place it on the farther edge of the table and yell, "*Pronto!*" A runner would appear. The runner would check the order slip, at which time the order was either slid into a white porcelain serving tray/plate or wrapped.

When the runner had to wrap the order, he'd scurry to a corner of the basement, where over the past several months Joe neatly stacked and stored newspapers. He would go back to the work table, spreading open the newspaper as he came (they'd always double or triple up on the newspaper sheets—a single sheet would not even last the trip up the creaky staircase). Then he would dump the contents of the pasta bowl into the proper spot (not the center) of the newspaper sheets, quickly and professionally wrapping them—south corner less than halfway up to north corner, getting the west side toward the east side, tucking the east over good, and rolling it all to the north. The men kept a spool (cone) of grocery store string beneath the worktable. The reaching down, the pulling, and the rolling of the package were done in what could be described as one fluid motion: a quick *pasticceria* knot, then snapping the string, tucking the package(s) under the arms, and starting for the steps, sans banister. At the bottom, they would shout, "Subway." Running up those stairs with an arm full, or coming down with more orders or a full pitcher of cold beer, was no place or time for a collision.

The area under most of the moaning and groaning staircase, and about double the area to the left, where Joe's would normally have ample room to store those beer kegs (wooden in those days) and extra blocks of ice, was another work area. Maybe in current restaurant parlance it would have been called "a prep area," but not at Joe's. Over time, this area became known as the Ice-a-Box-Sah (Ice Box).

Someone was always working in the Ice-A-Box-Sah. The meats were packed on ice, and most of the ice blocks were covered with a heavy canvas tarp. It was a tad cooler there, farthest from the oven. Another worktable occupied maybe 20 percent of the area. This was where they prepared the spits. Sometimes the spits would still be warm in spite of the water drum soaking.

The prep man would go and pick up an ample supply of spits, lay them carefully on his table's edge, and when ready or available, start to place the meat on them. There were always eight (four inch) pieces of sausage, or six lamb chops, or eighteen gnumariedi, all on their own separate spit. They were surgically stabbed right down the center, packed six inches away from the hilt and five inches from the point. Then with a quick and well-aimed dash of salt, the raw meat was then ready for the oven and another **"Pronto!"** shout thereafter.

This was the world that Fridone descended into.

He went immediately to the tosser. He whispered into his ear. The tosser nodded his acknowledgement and wrapped the next three gnumariedi packages for Fridone and placed them on a nearby stool. Fridone noticed that two beer pitchers by the oven were empty, so he shouted to Finnocchio and asked if he would take them upstairs for refills. The big man nodded, turned all the spits that were over the reddish and yellowish/orangish embers (occasionally one could see a burst of blue in there), and told the nearby spit stripper he'd be right back. If not, in five minutes the meats would be ready (*cinque minuto . . . sono pronto*). He picked up the two empties, just as Fridone was yelling, "Subway"; and he too started for the steps, up from the mine shaft. The burly big man followed under Fridone's green light, and those stairs seemed to creak and moan much deeper than just a few seconds ago. (It is said that muscle weighs more than fat.)

Fridone opted to go onto the customer side of the bar and easily hand Tony's uncles the three packages of gnumariedi, Finnocchio went on the service side of the long bar and stopped at the beer taps. He started filling one of the beer pitchers, nodding his hellos to Tony's uncles. Each of the uncles (and Fridone at his own insistence) placed a dollar and a half in front of Uncle Mike's narrow position at the bar. Dominic, with his right hand bouncing slightly, indicating it was enough, scooped up the quarters and the one dollar bill, turned, and played (what the paisano called) his Jewish piano. They would not let Peter contribute to the cost of the newspaper-wrapped packages, which (already) were starting to show the oil/grease seepage on the outside. Tony's people finished their beers and started back to the brownstone.

The gnumariedi was still warm, and the men could feel its warmth through the grease-stained newspaper.

Good old Fridone wished them well and a very good night and stepped into the bar position vacated by Mike. He caught Finnocchio's eye. They smiled and nodded—a smile and a nod that maybe only two bachelors could share and understand. Say what you may, even without a family (they'd frequent a "house" occasionally to satisfy their carnal needs), they were better off here in America than back in the old country. Their stomachs were seldom empty for very long; they had friends and piasanos, and the beer was cold.

Fridone watched his good friend fill the second pitcher of beer, wiping off the foam with one of the many available whale bones by the beer taps. He reached into his shirt pocket to pull out his last Parodi cigar. Cigar safely clutched between his teeth, he reached into the same pocket and pulled out a rectangular box of wooden matches that had a blue diamond with a red border on its face. The wording on the box said, "Diamond Matches," but Fridone could not read—Italian or English. Like he had done so many times before, in an act nearing an involuntary reflex, he adroitly snapped the red tip over the roughness of the striker, watched it burst into a red and yellow flame, waited a microsecond to let the sulfur burn out, and then placed the top of the flame to the bottom end of the cigar. He puffed, and the blue and white smoke accumulated around his face, almost making it disappear; slowly the cloud rose and dissipated. Old Fridone was taking a well-deserved break. Bull Dog, the sub bartender, gave him a beer.

Out of what seemed to be nowhere, a forestieri roughly grabbed Fridone's elbow, yanking it and twisting Fridone around so that they faced one another, and angrily demanded to know where his order was. The forestieri, from his seated position at one of the crowded bar room tables, had long ago placed his order and had just happened to witness Uncle Mike over the bar top conversing with Fridone. The forestieri had also watched Fridone's prompt delivery, and it immediately registered—he was a victim of preferential treatment. It was not fair! It was not just! Had he not been there so much longer than those four? Who does this little piece of junk think he's dealing with?

There was a different fairness and a different justice in East Utica in those days. And it only belongs to the beholder.

Finnocchio, carrying two full pitchers of beer, was heading back to the mine shaft; and his back was turned when Fridone was being manhandled. He casually shot a look over his left shoulder and in an instant saw and interpreted his old friend's dire predicament. The exact time from when the two sloshing beer pitchers touch the long mahogany bar top to the time Finnocchio's massive right hand clamped down on the back of the forestieri's neck is only a blur. His thumb and his long finger were on the neck and below both ears of the shocked and hurting forestieri.

"*Hay—ya! Che pesce se?* (What kind of fish are you . . . who do you think you are?)" It was an Old Italian expression, like the "patron saints" baggage of the immigrants, was incorporated into the vernacular and life of the neighborhood and all of East Utica. It was quickly and harshly said, seldom in jest, for it was always considered a serious and pending warning or challenge.

When Fridone's elbow was released, he stepped away from his tormentor, confused and a little frightened, his cigar falling from his mouth and landing near one of the spittoons. At first he found himself panting and staring wide-eyed at everything and nothing. Fridone shook his head as if to clear water from his ear. He saw the panic look in the forestieri's face, and he saw the fire in Finnocchio's eyes and quickly nodded he was okay. Finnocchio gave the forestieri a parting squeeze with that punishing right hand before jerking it loose with a snap of his thick wrist. The opening of that viselike death grip caused the stranger to gasp. He too stared wide-eyed.

Dominic stepped in, saying, "You are next. You are next . . . *sicuro*! Go sit down . . . You are next." The bewildered forestieri did return to his table. Dominic called one of the waiters over, gave him a liter bottle of wine, and told him to bring it to "that forestieri's table"—no charge.

At the table, the waiter opened the cork-screwed bottle, put a few drops into one of the four wine glasses he brought along, and offered it to the bruised patron.

His associates asked, "*Che successa?* (What happened?)" He replied, "*Niente* (Nothing)"; and he tasted the wine. He nodded approval to the waiter who in turn nodded back and then proceeded to fill all the other glasses. This time the waiter nodded to the group at the table, put the cork on the table to be examined and whiffed, (if so desired by anyone at the table), and returned to his regular dining room duties.

No charge. No trouble. Neither patron nor waiter once during the entire offering or acceptance exchanged words.

There was a different fairness and a different justice in East Utica in those days. And it did indeed belong to the beholder, but on that particular night, it also belonged to a four-and-a-half-year-old boy, his family, and *le su amici* (and their friends).

Gnumariedi and Last Glass

In groups of three and four, all the kids came back to Zia Chiara's flat. They were all silent, like when they entered a church, occasionally glancing at one another, unsure as whether to smile or cry. Tony was standing by his mother's side still kind of bewildered and amazed by all the activity. His brother Angelo, like going up to the altar rail to receive Holy Communion, slowly approached him and handed him his missing shoe. "I found it in the alleyway right by the concrete stoop," he quietly said.

Tony was still kind of bewildered and still amazed by all the activity, but now he was a lot happier. "Ma, look! Look! He found it! He found it!" His mother smiled, reached over, and affectionately rubbed his bother's curly hair and said, "Good boy, good boy."

The kids were not too sure of what to do or say, but *not those Italian mothers* in that room. Almost in unison, they snapped open their folded aprons and started issuing orders to their children. Tony's mother said to her older boys, "Go down to the cantina and get a quart of canned peaches and a quart of the canned plums and fill up the wine gallon." Aunt Lucy said to her older daughters Teresa and Frances, "Here is the key, go home and get that bag of lemons and bring the bag of sugar and some glasses." Aunt Grace said to Joey and Anthony, "Go out on to the porch and stoops and get the outside chairs." The other aunt Grace told Donetta to go with Zia Chiara to help her retrieve the food they had stored in the icebox earlier. She started to cut the bread. As the provolone was placed on the kitchen table, Zia Lucia started to cut it into thin triangular pieces and placed them on a plate. The big black olives were shaken out of the gallon tin and placed into a bowl. (Back in those days, you had to spit out the pit or gnaw around it like a chipmunk.)

Zia Lucia said, "Carmella run over and tell your sisters to give you the bread knife (always the sharpest in the home) and bring it to me." Zia Grazia (one and two) started to put out other serving platters. The dried, seasoned sausage and the pepperoni were expertly cut, very thin and very evenly; the trick, of course, was using the sharpest knife.

There is a maternal instinct prevalent in all ethnic groups—some believe more so with Mediterranean mothers: they know when kids are hungry. The lemons and sugar arrived. Tony's mom added the six she had to Zia Lucia's dozen. "We need another pitcher . . . Donetta, here's the key; go and get our two from the cup board . . . *fa subito!* (And hurry!)" Tony's mother started cutting and squeezing the lemons. The kids were going to have lemonade tonight. "Johnny, take this ice pick and chip off some ice from the big block in the icebox . . . be careful . . ." The kids were going to have really-really cold lemonade.

The long kitchen was mobbed, A beehive of activity. The kids were getting hungrier by each tick of that yellow clock on the shelf between the two large windows over the kitchen table, with lasso-twirling cowboy and horse figurine way above it all.

Enter four men with three newspaper-wrapped (sort of greasy) bundles of gnumariedi. All this almost became unbearable, especially for the kids. Some just remained *vocca aperto* (their jaws dropped open), awed. "Holy mackerel . . . can this be true?" others squealed with delight. Tony had not seen his father since about noon and when their eyes met, it was his father who smiled first and nodded as if to say, "Welcome home." (Home—a place you are protected, a place you protect.)

Time to organize. Break up the kids in groups of four, of various age strata, the eldest being in charge, with the strictest instruction to share and control and maintain order in the distribution of food and drink. The eldest were given a platter loaded with food and gnumariedi; another was given two full glass of lemonade to be shared with another group member (you drink from *dis* side, I'll drink from *dat* side); another, four bowls and a jar of canned fruit; and the youngest was given four forks and a *mop-pean* (dialect for either dish cloth or napkin), only one per group to be shared naturally!

The groups, one by one, left the kitchen and went out into the hall way, each seeking a camp site: sitting on the porch floor, another sitting on staircase steps (going up), another party of four finds camping area on steps that go down. It went like that. "Hey, watch it! Don't spill any lemonade."

The gnumariedi were still warm; the olives, salty and juicy; the provolone, sharp and tangy; the pepperoni, spicy and kind of soft; the dried sausage, spicier and a bit harder to chew; and the bread was crusty and good. One of the older cousins loudly asked the crowd in the hallway,

"Does the king of England eat better than this?"

"Nah! No way! Not in a zillion years."

The adults sat around the crowded table and also enjoyed their repast. "It was Michael's idea . . . he asked Fridone and we got them right away."

"Bravo, ah, Fridone, bravo!"

The next morning Fridone noticed bruises on his left biceps just above his elbow. A forestieri from Endicott had a stiff neck that lasted for a week or so and some slight bruises under each ear.

Tony went to his mother's side and asked if he could go out in the hallway with the other kids. Her first impulse was to deny the request, but a "look" from her older sisters and sister-in-law made her relent. She said, "Okay, but stay with Donetta; here, bring this to her group. And tell her to ask if any others want some more food." She gave Tony a soup bowl of gnumariedi. The boy held the bowl with both hands; he used his rump to open the screen door and went out into the hallway, looking for Antoinette. Tony's mother was trying to say thank you in still another way to Donetta.

The jarred fruit quarts were the first to empty, and the older kids drank the remaining sweet syrupy liquids right from the canning jars/quarts. The peach was sweeter. Those in charge of the eating parties started to come back into the kitchen, one after the other. They carried the empty platter with the four soiled forks carefully centered. The other two brought in the glasses, and the youngest in the party brought in the mop-peen. The older girls stayed in the kitchen. They would soon be needed. The older boys were told to take the little kids outside and play in the alleyway and—"*Per l'amore di Dio* (for the love of God)"—watch 'em!

Time to work. The food that remained was offered to Tony's aunts. All refused. The hot-water tank was lit. The mothers cleared the table, leaving only the wine glasses for the men and the wine gallon, which at the height of the activity was placed under the table on Tony's father's chair. Now that the kitchen table was cleared, the gallon was placed in its rightful place, the center of the table. (Immediately after the bottom of the gallon was wiped clean by the mop-peen) The wine glasses were all, once again, capped off and filled—"*ultima per la notte* (the last one of the night)."

Phone Call . . . Chewing Gum

The phone rang. It was Friday after 10:00 pm. Tony answered; it was Antoinette's son Anthony. "Yo . . . Ant—Knee . . . what's up? . . . Whadda ya doin'?"

There was a pause, then the reply which started with "Bad news." The bad news was relayed.

"No! No!"

Tony didn't know what to do; he just didn't know; instinctively and in his rage, he slammed the receiver back into its cradle. "No . . . No . . . ," he repeated to himself; his mind whirled; he stood there in front of the yellow kitchen-wall phone, not believing or not wanting to believe what he had just been told.

He had this not-so-rational thought: *It is the phone that brings the bad news . . . It is the phone! Punch it! Punch the fuckin' thing . . . It's gotta be destroyed . . . . No . . . No . . .*

how did it happen? It can't be true . . . some mistake . . . yeah, some mistake somewhere. It can't be true . . . It is the phone's fault . . . Punch it!

The phone rang again. It sounded as loud as the bongs of the yellow clock that looked like a miniature library sitting on a shelf in a kitchen between two large kitchen windows—the sounds that forced one to listen, calling him to tell him something. "What? . . . Time? . . . Yeah, sure . . . What is time? Whose time is it?" (Take a deep breath, deeper ; fill up your lungs, deeper.) It rang again. "Yeah, Ant-knee, . . . yeah, I heard ya . . . Sorry, must have gotten disconnected . . . Yeah, I heard you! . . . I told ya . . . must have gotten disconnected . . ."

"I'm coming home . . ."

"What? . . . No . . . no way! No . . . Fuck it . . ."

"I'm coming home . . . I'm coming home now! Did you tell my mother yet?"

"Oh . . . he did . . . and my sister in law is with them?"

"Okay . . . I'm coming up now . . . I should be there in three to three and half hours . . ."

"No!"

"I'm coming now!"

Tony went upstairs, told his wife the news. He put two extra twenties in his pocket and he left. His wife made him promise he'd call when he got there and told him to be careful. Tony said, "Yeah, okay." He was thinking, *I gotta get back . . . gotta go home . . . gotta get there now!*

If his green pickup were a horse, it would immediately recognize the oft traveled path. Up route 100, right on to 22, north again on the Turnpike, pay a toll at Clark Summit, charge on to Interstate 81, Binghamton, on to

Route 12, closing the gap to home. If the green pickup could sense it, she'd feel the intense urgency being applied by the ball of Tony's foot on the gas pedal. It was much firmer, much steadier than the other times driver and vehicle traveled along this familiar trail. *Gotta get home . . . Gotta get dare . . . 'snot gonna change nuttin' . . . dead is dead . . . but I gotta be there . . . I gotta give back . . . I might be needed . . . I gotta give back!*

When Tony gave up more than twenty-five years of smoking, he developed a quirky habit that manifested itself when driving and even more so when preoccupied with deeper thoughts. He would snap his fingers on his right hand, just his right hand and stare straight ahead, lost in those deep, dark thoughts. His wrist would hook over the top of the steering wheel, his hand loosely hanging, and one could easily hear the *snap, snap, snap, snap* coming from his hand and fingers. *Snap, snap, snap, snap.*

The alleyway was not too narrow, nor was it very wide. An automobile could not drive though it. The house on the west of the brownstone was a two-story frame and Goomba Nicolo and Commarre Margaretta were the proud owners. It had a peaked roof and imitation asphalt brick (red and black) siding. They had a backyard where he'd garden every summer, a fig tree he wrapped every November, and a grape arbor that shaded a homemade table all year round. Along with the homemade table were two brightly painted (green) City Parks Department benches. The benches were given to him long ago by an *amici* who wanted to repay a small favor. The benches looked just like the kind they had at Brandegee School playground. However, Brandegee School playground never reported any such property missing.

The alleyway between Tony's brownstone and Goomba Nicolo' s house was floored by a little bit less than four-by-four-foot concrete squares: two side by side, the entire length, passed the back alley stoop up to the garbage shed. The kids would play in there. The girls jumping rope, playing hopscotch; the younger boys (those not yet old enough to cross the street or go to the corner alone) playing sidewalk handball, or sitting on the stoop telling stories. It was a world within a world . . . with towering walls on each side that almost reached the sky.

On nice days, especially in the summertime, one could hear girlish voices echoing off the brownstone wall and Compare Nicolo's imitation brick walls, singing a cadence for the skip rope jumpers:

My mother gave me a nickel to buy a pickle
I didn't buy a pickle . . . I bought some chewing gum!
Ya da da da chewing gum
Ya da da da chewing gum
Ya da da da chewing gum
Ya da da da chewing gum

Tony watched Antoinette competing with another girl (from way over by Mount Carmel Church whose mother was a commarra to one of the tenants) in a serious skip rope jumping contest. Who was going to last the longest? "Ya da da da chewing gum, ya da da da chewing gum . . ." The skip ropes, fragments of a once-long powerful clothes line, snapping rapidly and violently on concrete alleyway square, were already starting to fray and began unraveling. Initially Tony would blink when the rope snapped on the concrete, but before long he'd only be staring at the spot the rope beat against the concrete. It was no contest; nobody could beat Antoinette, nobody. She was the best on the block, the best in the world! If you'd look closely, you could see that tiny beads of sweat formed on the pores of her kind of flat, wide nose. Itsy-bitsy tiny beads. She panted slightly and caught Tony's admiring stare and secretly smiled at him. It was the kind of smile that started slowly, tugging at the left side of her lips and then blossoming into something really special. She only smiled at Tony. To smile at her former opponent would be bragging or showing off. An unwritten social and moral code was practiced. It was enough that she won. Who benefits if she gloats?

"Gotta get back . . . Gotta go home . . . Gotta try to give back . . . Gotta get there . . . now!" The cab of the pickup was suddenly illuminated bright red and sort of blinking. "Oh shit . . . a cop . . . where the hell did he come from?"

It was after midnight. (He's not *gunna* give you a break.) "Eat this pound of shit, get your ticket, and get *odda* here . . ."

Spare me the lecture, asshole. "Gotta get home . . . I am needed there . . . *Gotta* get going . . . How important is it to know what five times nine times three equals? '*S not* important . . . *Gotta* get home . . . *Dat's* important . . . *Gotta* give back . . . Fair is fair . . . *Gotta be dare now!"*

Winding Clock . . . Funeral

Page Up

Soon there was neatness and order in Ma's kitchen. The aunts took off their aprons, folded them neatly, and returned to the table. Eventually someone said, "*è tarda* (it is late)," as if on cue; the miniature library-looking yellow clock struck a quarter of an hour. "The kids are tired!" The mothers nodded, showing agreement. One of the uncles said, "*è vera . . . siamo pronto?* (it is true . . . are we ready?) Get the kids . . . *adiamo* (let's go)." Uncle Dan, Aunt Grace, and Antoinette were the last to leave. Carrying the two glass pitchers, and being the last one out, and kind of reminiscing on what a day it had been, Antoinette forgot; she reached back quickly but was just a split-second late; the screen door slammed. She quickly apologized to Zia Chiara, and as quick as that apology was offered, her aunt assured it wasn't anything. None of the aunts wanted to hear their screen door slam; from an early age all of the kids were reminded/scolded/cajoled and threatened not to slam the screen door. Ah, but does one think Donnetta could have done anything wrong in the eyes of her aunt that night, or any other night in the many years to come?

None of those kids, none of the adults would ever completely forget that long day. True, each would probably remember one thing and another maybe something else; but they would remember something. That memorable day became a family reference point in the years to come. "Naw . . . Naw . . . Commarra Gemma died right after we lost little Tony . . ." or "Sure she was there . . . don't you 'member? She was sitting on the stoop by Joe the Barber's corner where we found Tony . . ." or "These gnumariedi taste almost as good as the ones we had when Tony got lost . . ."

The family slept well that night. In Tony's flat, the yellow clock with the lasso-twirling cowboy on a rearing steed, on a shelf between two large windows, ticked as loud as it wanted, sounded the quarter and half hours with single gong and, on the hour, gave full the count. The next morning, as Tony's mother was making his father's lunch, Tony's father positioned one of the kitchen chairs between the two large windows, stepped up on it, placed the special clock key into a little hole on the white face of the clock (between the III and the VI), and twisted the key. He'd do that every morning, wind the clock.

Page Down

Tony always liked going back to his old parish, St. Anthony of Padua. Everything was always so familiar and different to him at the same time. Tony would notice the small changes: "Oh yeah, that used to be blue or that was the cross that hung over the altar before the ecumenical conference. Most of the statues did not change their positions in years. Santo Rocco is still in his glass-encased quasi-shrine just to your left as you come in through the double door north entrance, and before you go through the swinging doors into the church. Santo Rocco, pastoral staff in hand, is still looking skyward, still pointing to the bloody wound on his thigh. An animal standing by his wounded leg. Santo Rocco, the patron saint of Logorotorndo.

Tony was baptized here in Saint Anthony of Padua Church, as were his brothers and most . . . not all . . . of his American born-cousins. It was a city parish, with a bell tower, and it had only one large bell that pealed to announce Sunday morning masses and the Agnus Dei daily at noon. You could hear it on the nine hundred block of Catherine; you could also hear bells from Our Lady of Mount Carmel, St. Agnes, and St. Stanislaus.

Tony's mother would often comment on how "different" or how "foreign" suburbia living was especially on Sunday mornings. She'd say to him, "You can't tell if it is a Sunday: nobody seems to dress up, the kids don't look special, I don't hear any bells, somebody cuts the grass, somebody washes clothes, it is like any other day. Not like Sunday."

And Tony would tease her by replying, "That's why I bring you down here for two or three weeks so that you can make the kitchen smell like meatballs and sauce on Sundays."

His mom used to tell him that St. Anthony's Church was built in the early twenties. When Zia Lucia married, the ceremony was held in the basement of the church. The super structure of the church had not yet been completed. Zia Lucia and her husband married in November 1922. Tony makes a distinction between what he calls suburbia Catholic churches and city parishes. The suburban is too sterile for him, too plain, too much like an auditorium—stadium setting. Are those the Stations of the Cross or not?—just too plain. Cost effective? Maybe, but they are not the *houses of worship* that would make him want to believe. No statues, no racks of burning candles (a nickel each), no unpadded kneelers, no little black spring-loaded hat holders screwed on the backside of the pew that would click loudly if he were not careful. None of that stuff. How could it be God's house? He always liked going back to his old parish—St. Anthony of Padua at Bleecker and St. Anthony Streets.

But today, today he was there for a sad occasion—much sadder reason. The sealed casket in the middle of the aisle—with the white cloth draped over it, with its prominent red cross—contained the remains of his beloved Donnetta. Tony's mother was given a place of honor, standing between Antoinette's two sons in the first pew. Small tired old woman, who saw so much in a very hard life, was kneeling and whispering, "May the souls of the faithful departed rest in peace . . ."

Tony, with only his wife by his side, sat behind Antoinette's sons and her grandchildren and his two older brothers five pews back. The church was packed (by funeral standards anyway) with relatives and friends. Not bad for "just another factory girl . . . and the best skip rope jumper on the block . . ."

Soon the Mass was over. The funeral directors were turning the casket, and Tony remembered his mother telling him as a child the deceased entered the church head first and always left feet first. Tony thought to himself, *Well, Nan* (a nickname he came to call her over the years), *this is the last time you leave St. Anthony.* He recalled her wedding day, a clear cold day in early December and how she was smiling coming down this very aisle. He remembered he once saw male parishioners pushing and steering the statues of Saints Cosmo and Daminio down the very same aisle, taking them out for the Sunday afternoon street procession.

They all stood. The pallbearers walked along side of the casket down this very aisle—solemn young men. Antoinette's sons placed Tony's mom between them and started to follow, their wives and children stepped into this very aisle. Then the organist played "**Tu Scendi Dalle Stelle.**" The family always sang that song on Christmas Eve, "**la viglie de natale**."

The Italian Christmas carol, the lyrics, the sweet familiar-sounding music—a flood of memories—just overwhelmed Tony. He closed his eyes tightly; tears started escaping; he saw Antoinette again smiling that beautiful smile, ladling the traditional Christmas wedding soup into the waiting bowls, smiling, passing it to the right and left, making sure everyone got a lot of little meatballs, some escarole, some chunks of white chicken breast, joking, and happy to have her family around her and at her table.

And for the second time in his life—first time when his father died—Tony slowly slipped, maybe melted would be more accurate, to his knees on the church-pew kneelers of his St. Anthony of Padua Church, and he wept. Elbows on the back of the pew in front of him, his face—cheeks and eyes—covered by his big hands like trying to stop and force back the flood of tears, he wept openly, loudly, and without shame, as bitterly as St. Peter did on Good Friday.

"God loves me . . . God loves you . . . who cares what nine times six plus seventeen equals to? Who cares? 'S *not* important . . . I tried to be smart . . . just couldn't . . . yeah! Me too . . . It's okay . . . 's *not* important . . . You just *gotta* be good and you *gotta* love more than you hate . . . You *gotta* be good . . . You were a good girl . . . a good woman . . . God loves you . . . God loves me . . . *Dat's* what's important. It's not just being smart."

The Economy

Barbeque Cop
Lunch Pail
Bean Picking . . . Summer Job
The Game . . . The Boss
Fridone's Acceptance
Full Tray . . . Finocchio's Dilemma
The Pig Could Do It
The Fight . . . The Stop Sign

Barbeque . . . Cop

Like a thousand years ago, when Tony transferred out of the Utica area, he and his wife "worked" at being accepted in their new locale; he did not want his family to be considered *forestieri* (his youngest was not yet in school); he wanted the kids to feel that they belonged, and although the family unit was much less (only the five of them—no cousins, no aunts, no uncles, no grandparents living nearby), they were first and foremost an Italian family. That is the way Tony thought: an army of five, whose motto was Family and Food. Everything else was secondary; they gave each other strength and were strengthened in return.

They have an annual festival feast in a nearby community, and through the efforts of a friendly mailman, Tony and his wife were coaxed into volunteering. That was thirty years ago. They don't mind it, as a matter of fact, and over the years they worked as a team and made many friends and met new acquaintances. Admittedly some were better than others, but their base grew and compounded with the neighborhood expansion, school, Little League, nursery schools, Cub Scouts, etc. Tony and his wife did what they set out to do. Become accepted. In Tony's mind (and thank God not in his kids' nor his wife's way of thinking) in the "suburbia/development" environment he'd always remain a forestierei; but *dats* all right so long as the family is safe and healthy.

Back to the festival. The latest one, Tony and his wife were working the barbeque area/stand. They provided aprons for the volunteers. It was always a test (maybe "challenge" would be a better word) for Tony, that foolish long white apron—and its "shrinking" drawstring. He eventually came to figure it out: if he was under 240 pounds, he could tie the apron string himself and in the front. If not, he'd have to ask his wife to tie it in the back, as he had to do this year. He remembered his mother and his aunts snapping their homemade aprons, cleaning it of crumbs or lint or anything, then neatly folding them, about the size of an eight-by-ten envelope, placing them directly in front of them on the kitchen tabletop, interlacing their fingers and placing their hands dead center over the apron like it was going to fly away or something like that—it was just an apron.

What strong and resourceful women they were! What courage they possessed to do so much with so little! Who works more or harder, a mother of three or six or eleven, or a Park Avenue female single-parent attorney with a Hispanic cleaning lady and an oriental cook? Who gives more? Who takes more out of the system? Who contributes more? For all his rhetoric, Tony didn't know, could not even guess—just too many variables in there. It is progress. Who is it, the French (?)—that say the more things change, the more they stay the same.

But sometimes he would think, *What happens to the family unit? Ma was "home." Yeah, I know . . . but now it becomes part of today's parlance, "Not the amount o time but the quality of time . . . ," they say . . . but sumptin' bout quality time" . . . it ain't 24-7 . . . not like Ma who was always in the kitchen.*

When alone, and his thoughts drifted that way, a wisp for smoke far back in his gray cells would rise like a warning, a warning not to go there: "You're too excitable.

you go there . . . and you open your big mouth. The smart kids will burn ya! And ya end up telling yourself, 'I should've said . . . or . . . why didn't I remember . . . next time . . . next time.' There are few, if any, next times. Ya gotta learn to think before you say something. Them smart kids will burn ya, shame ya, yeah . . . that's the word, 'shame on ya . . . like ya never gunna be smart . . . ya never . . . ever . . . will win an argument . . . or persuade the smart ones . . ."

When all that self-inflicted mental punishment was done, Tony would just quietly ask himself, "Yeah, but . . . does that really make me wrong? Does that make abortion okay? I was in high school before I realize that a Trojan was a Greek citizen. Does it make gay marriages right? Is that in the natural order of things? A test tube is what . . . ? The nth degree of that is no promulgation of the species . . . What is a thoroughbred and what is a cur . . . ?" Then that wisp of smoke . . . and Tony would think, *Don't go there . . . you ain't smart enough . . . keep your mouth shut . . . tend to your family . . . you don't have to prove yourself smart . . . even if you are smart in a couple of things . . . it is what you feel, and do that. That is what makes you what you are.*

Page Up

They went to the Rialto Theater. "Red River" was playing: John Wayne and Montgomery Clift. ("How come the mayor-I-cans call their kids names like Montgomery? Did ya ever hear of a St. Montgomery? Did ya ever? Me neither!") Tony and the other guys watched the spectacular stampede scene. That big sliver screen filled up with longhorns running as fast as they could, running, running in a tight pack as fast as they could, their snouts sometimes close to the ground. Other times pointed skyward, running as fast as they could. Where are they going? What are they thinking? Fear? Whadda dey scared' bout? Their huge heads swinging from left to right . . . right to left as far as they could . . . if they could . . . up and down . . . wide-eyed . . . looking at everything and seeing nuttin'. What if one stumbles, ain't nobody gunna stop or slow up or help or nuttin'? Just runnin' as fast as they can . . . mooing and moaning . . . kicking up dust . . . afraid and runnin'. Their mudders and fadders are in there . . . their brothers and sisters . . . runnin' . . . runnin' . . . in a tight pack.

Later, when Tony found himself in the sanctuary of his tenement flat and his ma was shelling dried fava beans, and his pa reading the "Il Progresso," he told them about the stampede scene. He described it as best he could and asked if they thought there were mother cows and father cows and brother and sister cows in the pack and if they were running together or separate or what. He wanted to know if they knew one another in that race to nowhere and if his ma thought they'd get together afterwards. His ma said, "Sono creatura de Dio. (They are creatures of God but not people.) Noi abbiamo anima! (We have a soul!)." His pa looked up from his newspaper, smiled and nodded a yes to Tony. Tony knew it had to be true, and said, "That's why we're better than animals. I'm family, I belong, I am part of sumptin' bigger than I am."

In his white starch apron, Tony and his wife worked the barbeque table. The work table was tucked away in the southeast corner of the huge pavilion, the perimeter of which was a counter top. Cashier strategically placed midway and in the corners. Runners coming and going to the various food tables and then delivering orders. Next to the barbeque table (the barbeque kept warm in large roasters) was the hotdog and hamburger grills. During the course of the evening, two bicycle police leisurely patrol through the crowd. Tony just can't get used to cops on two-wheeled bikes—they look like what? (Don't go there! They are on the job; let it go.)

They decided to take a break near the south/east corner of the pavilion. One of the police officers took off her riding helmet, regally placing it in the crux of her left arm (like a knight dismounting from his steed) and entered the pavilion. She knew a senior volunteer worker and they struck up a conversation. Tony looked over his barbeque table and kind of studied the presence of the law. Spandex black shorts, white short-sleeve shirt (open at the collar) expensive black-and-white sneakers, and attached to her belt a nine-millimeter Glock, a radio, cuffs, and a night stick.

She had a tattoo above her left ankle, just above the sock line—exposed. With a smirk, Tony thought, *Whadda picture of motherhood . . . she probably threw a javelin in high school . . . wonder if'n she ever read Steinbeck's* Grapes of Wrath *and the closing scene: the beast feeding and . . . what? . . . WHAT YOU THINK . . . motherhood s'posed t' be? . . . Don't go dare! . . . they'll burn ya! . . . Don't go dare!* The smirk left his face.

The crime buster's friend brought her a hamburger (no money exchanged) and they chatted. Tony's Uncle Dan never liked it when cops would come into his bakery, get some bread, and never offer to pay—at least offer, damn it! (You got a job.) Tony smirked and reminded himself,

Not all things are changing . . . and . . . the more things change, the more they stay the same.

He wondered if that tattoo made the "law" tougher, as tough as his aunt Lucy or tougher than either one of his aunt Graces? He didn't think so. A wisp of smoke appeared and Tony reminded himself not to go there: *And all you got to do is protect the sanctity of the family . . . your family!* He then pondered, *Are we leaving the cave or are we returning to the cave? Don't go there! Do you smell that wisp of smoke? Let it go. BUT? Are we returning to men running around with clubs and women huddling in caves trying to keep their children alive? Are we moving forward or back ward to test-tube babies . . . genetic changes . . . body and mind perfect . . . with or without love . . . with or without a sense of belonging . . . meaning of history? Don't go there . . . yeah . . .*

"How many barbeques did you say? Gotcha! . . . Coming right up!"

And he thought, *Yeah, but does a tattoo really make her tougher? Any better?*

Lunch Pail

Page Up

When Tony was still dreaming and constantly badgering his mother for his very own wagon, he recalled that one day when his father had returned from work and quietly spoke to his mother. His father asked his mother to see if she could save some money, a dollar or a dollar and a half so that he could buy a metal lunch pail. His mother replied, "Secura, ma perche?" (Of course, but why?) His father explained that those sewer rats (those big ugly bastards) in the textile mills could easily eat through the brown paper bags he was using to carry his lunch. Tony's mother gasped—the thought/sight of it took her breath away. His father went on to explain, as they had done for the past few days, he would put his lunch into Don Alberto's lunch pail. His father said that when Don Alberto became aware of his dilemma he immediately offered to share his all-metal lunch pail. His father did not wish to impose on Don Alberto's kindness any more than necessary. Don Alberto did not mind sharing the protection at all; you see—he too was once hungry and deprived.

(You have to understand that Don Alberto was a true and just and honorable man.) He had once studied in a Sicilian seminary in the Old Country. When he passed on, Tony's parents had a Mass said for him—not a weekday Mass but a Sunday High Mass with three priests at 11:00 AM. The year before he died, at Christmastime, Tony made him a Christmas card—a very crude piece of art, a snowman with a top hat and black coal buttons and what may have been a broom.

Tony reminded his mother to put his card in his father's lunch pail the next morning. He didn't want his father to forget to deliver it. He genuinely liked Don Alberto and still remember him walking up Kossuth Avenue, smoking a crooked pipe, creating a cloud of smoke around his face and waving and smiling to little fat Tony. His father told him that Don Alberto was delighted with the card and showed all the coworkers on their lunch break. It made Tony feel good.

Page Down

A lifetime later, Tony and his wife gave the two boys who lived next door to them a tray of homemade cookies. The boys beamed with delight. His wife made them pick out the cookies that they liked; and Tony lit up the Christmas tree for them and they ashed. Tony told them, "I had never had an artificial tree . . . simply because I liked the smell and the feel of a 'real tree.' So what if there are a couple of pine needles on the floor . . . ? So what? And one more thing, boys . . . a real tree doesn't have to be perfect . . . What is perfect, anyway? If your fresh cut tree is lacking . . . you make it perfect . . . by trimming and decorating . . . right?"

The wide-eyed boys left his home, but only after saying their thanks and expressing their appreciation, and walked to their own home next door. About a half hour later, the younger boy was back, ringing the doorbell. Tony answered.

The boy gave him a homemade Christmas card. Tony thanked him profusely; the boy smiled and ran home A few minutes later, the doorbell rang again. Tony was upstairs and his wife answered. It was the other brother, and he too had a homemade Christmas card.

When Tony came back downstairs, both Christmas cards were on the kitchen table; he picked them up, studied them, and smiled. His wife said, "Cute, aren't they? Put them in the Laugenburg there! (A brand name for an artsy-fartsy manufacture of basket collectibles . . . she liked to collect) Put them in along with the others cards."

"Naw . . ." Tony said, "I'm gonna take these upstairs and put them in my computer room."

"Why in the world would you want to do that?"

He answered, "'S not important."

Bean-picking Summer Job

Page Up

Long ago

. . . . 900 block of Catherine Street . . . .

About 7:00AM in the early warmth of a cloudless July morning, sitting on the stoop of a Catherine Street brownstone, waiting for the bus to go bean picking, watching "that" old lady hawking produce from her pushcart, she used to smoke Italian stogies—Di Napoli or were they Parodi?—right there on the street! I don't think my mother or my aunts ever got over this shameful public display although it probably did not deter sales, especially if the prices were right. She used to tie the catalonia in neat bunches about the size you can make when showing a circle with your hands; then she'd stand them like tall green soldiers into a large white enamel wash basin—the cut ends were submerged in about two inches of water to keep the "life" in them. "Guardare come sono bella!.(Three for dime . . . Not a penny less!)" Make a sale. Hawk your produce, lift the rear bar of the old pushcart, move on down to Pellettieri Avenue then Jay Street. Yell what you have in your pushcart. Yell so they can hear you in the rear flats and the upper flats of the brownstones, singing out loudly.

"*Catalonia . . . bella . . . pomidoro . . . bella . . . rosso . . . bella . . .*"

The two large iron spoke wheels of the pushcart squealed and sang the harmony.

The middle of summer, maybe a little after 7:00PM, Tony's peer group, in pairs or alone, all seemed to gravitate to the rear stoop at the end of the brownstone's alleyway. They had all eaten supper at home and were allowed out. Their sisters would follow shortly after the dishes were washed, dried, kept, and the rug shaken out and the floor swept. ("Yeah but . . . *dey* didn't *haf da* go down the cellar to get the wine or the quarts of tomatoes or take out the garbage . . . or stuff like *dat!*") The older boys, maybe twelve and older, those who have already been confirmed by the bishop, most of them having received their first wristwatch as a gift, which they proudly wore when they went down to the corner at Roxies Candy Store. (If they wore their watches, they'd better not be late coming home.)

Tony's group sat on the three concrete steps of the rear stoop, sometimes as many as four of them on each of the three cool concrete steps at the threshold of the tenement. Court was held, and reports of the day were presented.

Carmella, one of Tony's older cousins, picked eighteen bushels of beans today, the most of anyone in the Western's Bean-picking gang. It was the first pick in that field and the bean plants were loaded. Her hands could fly; while still on her bony knees she'd pick a bush clean, then reach for the bushel's two wired handles (which as the bushel filled with beans became heavier and the wire would always seem to cut into her palms and fingers), lift the basket, and move it forward a foot or so, then vigorously attacking the next bean plant, which soon became stripped of it's fruit. When the basket was filled, she got up to go get an empty bushel basket from one of the tall stacks of empties strategically placed throughout the bean field.

If needed, (should they fail to notice) Carmella would call for her younger brothers Sammy and Anthony to carry the basket to the scales. Sometimes the "Straw Boss" would be a black adult male who had been a "permanent" migrant worker for the Western family. The straw boss would weigh the bushels. If the far end of the pointed balance bar rose and struck the top of the balance—"O ring!"—hard and remained there, he'd reach in with his large hands, scoop out some beans, hold them in his hands, and watch the balance point move downward until it sort of floated in the center. Should the pointed arrow end of the balance bar not move when the basket would be placed on the scale's platform, the straw boss would take the bushel off the scale and tell you to go get more beans.

If it weighed enough, he'd give you a green theater-type ticket with a redeemable value of fifteen cents. ("A *lotta* beans . . . but . . . , boy, could her hands fly!")

Anthony, the elder, would hold the ticket firmly between his thumb and forefinger, almost pinching the hell out it. He'd stuff his homemade handkerchief (and his brother's too) into the front left pocket of his bib overalls. Sammy, who had interlaced his fingers and now cradled the surplus beans (if any) against his stomach, was ready to go back. They'd walk back under the hot July sun to where the rest of the family was picking. Anthony would give the ticket to the eldest sister, Lucy, who would proudly yell the total count so far and announce how close they were to a new record.

Anthony would give his brother back his handkerchief. The boys had used them to cover the cutting wire handles of the basket when they carried it to the weigh station, to the straw boss, and to the waiting trucks. The excess beans that Sammy carried back into the picking field were like a dividend to the younger boys. They were equally divided and deposited into their own baskets that didn't nearly ever fill as quickly as Carmella's. They'd kneel down on the ground (steering away from any stones) and then started picking the beans again.

But their hands did not fly like Carmella's. All the kids decided long ago it was much more financially beneficial to keep Carmella picking as long as possible. Her hands would fly. Sure, just another factory girl quitting school in the seventh grade, but her hands could fly; and should she be on "piece work" in a local textile mill, she'd easily exceed the rate.

All of the bean pickers had their own two-gallon zinc pail. When they left in the morning, they'd have a couple of sandwiches, a sweater (if it got cold or started to rain), and a hat (to keep the murderous sun off their heads). Water, sometimes cold, was provided by the farmers in large milk cans. At the end of the workday, most of the pickers would half-fill the zinc pail with handfuls of fresh beans and "secretively and cleverly" cover the beans with their sweaters and board the truck (in the earlier days) or the bus (in later days) and go home. The fresh beans were still another dividend or *benie*; they ate a lot of fresh green beans in the summer. (Ma would also can some for winter.)

The kids would sing songs and occasionally shout insults to other kids that just hung around the street corners on the ride home. Some of the kids thought, *This was still better than school* . . . , but not all of them.

But they'd always sing.

On Sunday mornings, the Westerns and the Argentos and other farmers would come to designated street corners in the various neighborhoods and redeem the little green theater-type tickets. The cold hard cash always helped, especially when Pa wasn't working a full week. If Ma couldn't go to the designated corner to "redeem" the little green theater tickets, she would send her two eldest.

"Wow! Eighteen bushels!" And the kids would sing on the way home.

(On the stoop, some *'portant stuff,* some *stuff nuttin' special,* sitting, *tellen',* making their History, *tellen' dreams).*

Another one of Tony's cousins and a peer, Joe, asked, "Wanna know what happen today at Goomba Joe's Restaurant just now . . . just before I went home to eat? Joe did not go picking, although his sisters and brother did. Joe, mostly through the efforts of an aggressive and outspoken father, (Tony's Uncle Mike) secured a full-time summer job at Goomba Joe's Restaurant and on school days, three-thirty to six-thirty and all day Saturday. During the summer he'd get a lunch, and a lunch every Saturday year round, and four dollars every week in the summer and two dollars and fifty cents during the school year.

He worked, but he did not sing on the way home. He swept the floors; he took out the garbage; he stacked the soda and beer empties; when needed, washed dishes; cleaned the toilets; he neat-folded paper napkins, like when one made a triangular paper airplane with its sharp nose point. He'd place the napkins into clean Pilsener-shaped beer glasses and set them out onto the eating tables (front room and the back room), washed the windows, scrubbed dirty tables, occasionally clean someone's vomit. He would go around the neighborhood barbershops, butcher shops, and any place where they got a daily newspaper. He would collect yesterday's paper and then store them in Joe's gold mine for future use.

But what he hated the most the very, very, most was dumping and cleaning the spittoons. It had to be done twice a day, at noon, and just before he went home. He would gag, breathe through his mouth, looking in the opposite direction as he dumped the contents of the spittoon into the toilet or the trough. He would rinse the lid and the bas under the full force of the water tap then sneak a look to make sure there was nothing left inside it. True, he was not out in the hot sun, but he paid for it in a cruel and a humiliating way. No, Joey didn't sing on the way home; and it wasn't because he was alone either.

"What happen, Joe? Tell us . . . !"

Like one of those magical moments that you relish, that you want to live forever and ever and ever, Joe had center stage—**FRONT**.

The Game . . . The Boss

"What happen? . . . Joe, tell us! . . . Tell us . . ."

A dramatic and theatrical pause. The cluster of boys waited; it got quiet; those who could twisted and turned their heads to look right at Joe. Others cocked their heads, pointing one of their ears to the place where Joe was sitting and listened with all their might.

Joe lowered his voice slightly. Tony could hear the air whistling up through his nostrils when he inhaled, then Joe slowly and deliberately scanned his audience, all of them and said, "Finnocchio almost killed Donato, 'the Bulldog' tonight!"

"What? What? What?"

"If Joey didn't have it before, he sure as heck had theirs undivided now. Finnocchio could kill a hundred bulldogs if he wanted . . . a hundred . . . easy . . . !"

Everybody knew Finnocchio, one of the bachelors that lived at Zio Pasquale's boarding house on Broad Street—big, strong guy, a giant who worked at the Utica Boiler Works-Foundry. On workdays, at four or four thirty, he'd walk all the way from around Proctor Park/Culver Avenue straight to Joe's Restaurant. He would belly up to the bar and immediately down three or four cold tap beers. (The beer was always cold and good at Joe's because he stored all the kegs in the cellar/mine. Cooled by the fifty-pound blocks of ice on them, and further, the coils at the bar were always packed with chunks of ice. It was Joe's and Dominick's practice to flush and clean the coils every Monday morning.)

Everyone who knew Finnocchio knew that the first couple of beers were his way of washing out the foundry dust from his mouth. He'd take big mouthfuls, swish it around, and swallow. At one time during this cleans in ritual, he would reach back into his rear pocket and pull out a large red or blue bandanna. His nostrils also had to be purged and cleaned; this was done very loudly and very thoroughly. The regular patrons came to accept and eventually came to accurately call this habit Finnocchio's trumpet call.

The nostril blasting/cleaning would go to at least three fanfares. After each, Finnocchio would examine the deposit in the bandanna, looking for black dust particles trapped in the mucus. Usually by the third exam, there were none. Dominick or Joe would give him a clean white towelette (not a conventional napkin size but larger—napkins were much too small; paper napkins were out of the question) and he would take this dishcloth with him into the men's restroom.

In the far corner of the restroom, by the toilet, was a small wash basin with only one tap (cold water). Sometimes, but not always, there'd be a bar of Lava soap—more sand than soap. Finnocchio would strip to his waist and start to soap and wash his massive upper body. (Maybe sand his upper body would be more correct.) If there wasn't any Lava soap, Finnocchio would use the Dutch Cleanser (with that Dutch woman in her bonnet and with a stick, chasing dirt). The cylindrical cleanser box was always on the floor, near and under the toilet tank.

By now, Finnocchio's mouth was washed out with beer, his nostril blasted clean, and his upper body, although a little raw, maybe reddish in spots, was cleansed. He dried himself off with the towelette and carefully pulled up his union underwear top and put on his shirt and pulled up and adjusted his suspenders.

He was proudest of his clean hands. An hour ago, the Devil himself would have looked away from his dirty hands, not now. He patted the few long strands of hair on his shining dome, to the left—he was not vain, nor was he messy. He looked again at his clean hands and left the men's restroom. He remembered his mother years and years ago, telling him "if you are going to eat bread . . . because bread is holy . . . give God your clean hands to break the bread . . . bread is holy."

He had snapped the dishcloth after the heavy use, slightly feeling the moisture forced away from it, folded it in half and walked to the bar to retrieve his lunch pail. He spotted an empty table, asked Dominick for a pitcher of beer. The lunch pail went onto the left far corner of the table; he went back for the pitcher and a glass, put the towelette on the table (it will from then on be used as a *mop-pean* (a napkin), and he was ready to eat.

Joe's kitchen wasn't that big; it had a door way (the door itself long removed for safety and speed), and on the wall facing the bar dining tables, had a four-by-six service window. Finnocchio would look through the serving window and ask Joe what he was serving. Normally it would be a two-plate choice: pasta fagioli, pasta ceech, pasta piselli, rigatoni with a braciola, catalions. Joe had some nice roasted peppers today; one of the farmers sold him a basket earlier in the day. Food stuff that would stick to your ribs. Finnocchio would make his choice.

All the boys on the rear alley stoop knew that Finnocchio had not just one heaping plate full of whatever but two!—and at least one loaf of bread; the kitchen did not have to cut the bread, he preferred to reverently and slowly pull it apart. His hands were clean. The boys knew all this because Joey told them (and you don't ever lie about things like that).

Earlier that afternoon, some of the old-timers started playing cards at Joe's. It was either briscoe or scopa (sweep), card games that came from the old country. The eights, nines, and tens were not used in either game. Both were always played with partners. In scopa the seven of diamonds was always a point card; the team with the most tricks also got a point (count) as well as the team with the most diamonds. If one of the teams had at least three sevens, it'd be another point (*primeer*). One could also score a point if he was able to pick the last card off the center of the table—that was a scopa. When one had a scopa, he'd place the one card face up in the stack of his already played cards so he wouldn't forget and also to remind his opponents he was winning.

Briscola was Tony's favorite. The ace was worth eleven; the three worth ten; king, three; queen, two; and the jack, one. Everyone was dealt three cards to start; the thirteenth card off the deck was placed face up, and its suit would be trump. When someone led, another had to follow suit or trump it. The person who won the trick would then be the first to pick off the stack that anchored the trump suit card and then lead.

The strangest thing about that game was that absolute silence had to be maintained during the first trick. Thereafter, one was allowed to send code words to his partner: "Can you watch? Maybe . . . you got a card, dick? (points) . . . I got balls . . ." and so on. On the final hand, when all the cards were picked off the table, the partners would hand each other their cards, study them, and return them. So in reality, of the twelve cards left to be played, one would know what and where seven were.

Without anyone in particular asking, Joey said, "They were playing scopa since about two o'clock."

Little Sammy asked, "How big was the pot?" One didn't have to be an adult to know that stuff.

As the games progressed during the afternoon, two tables were going, one of which was directly under the black-and-white ceiling fan that was starting to hum a little bit. Dominick told Joey, "After the game or before you go home, squirt some oil up there and cover the table good." Joey did that before and it required him to not only stand on one of the tables, but also an empty wooden Coca-Cola soda case. Joey would dutifully put newspaper on the chair and table, complete the task, and then remove the case, the papers and wipe down both seat and table.

Regardless of the slight hum, it was comfortable there. It was cool and with the front screen door opened, more fresh air came inside. It was as good as it was going to get. There were eight players at two tables and other patrons (most of them standing at the bar occasionally using either the foot rest or the spittoons) all of whom either drank wine or beer. Occasionally, one would order a side plate of those great-smelling peppers with some bread or a heaping plate of black olives—with bread.

When a team acquired enough points (usually twenty-one), that particular game was over and the losing team contributed a quarter (each) to the pot. The house furnished the tables with two empty Medalia D'Oro coffee cans for the pot money. In time the irony of the name on those coffee cans and the improvised service they preformed would become recognized. It was kind of a busy afternoon, with the various players and patrons and all.

The players: Bull Dog, who had kind of a "city job" and seldom worked in the afternoons; Zio Rocco, who was known to have sired seven sons and his sons all had seven kids, and he was considered the fountain head of all the Garramone west of the Mississippi. He was the eldest; in his old age he was "kept" by his single daughters (who all worked at the various textile mills in the neighborhood) and a single son who was to be married shortly. All of his sons (like his daughters) worked—and worked hard.

There was "Rockzees," whose wife took over their candy store at 1:00PM till closing at 9:00PM. There was Fat John who worked nights (eleven to seven) and his wife worked days and his kids all went bean picking. There was Rick-Coo-Cho, who wasn't too nice a guy. His daughters worked and he'd open their pay envelopes at the end of the week and took what he wanted or thought he needed. His wife would do some seamstress work. The story goes; he once took his mistress up into his third-floor cold-water flat, with his wife and kids there and took *la puttana* (the whore) into his bedroom and he closed the door.

There was Papa Tony, a nice old guy who recently moved up from West Virginia, with his son and his American daughter-in-law and two grandsons. Talk was he came up with a lot of money, bought a three-story brownstone (six families, communal toilet on each level) and he lived off the rent. He shared a ground-level flat with his son and his family. No rent was charged to the son, but he and his boys would do the maintenance.

Joey said there were others, especially later when the Oneita and Mohawk textile mills let out after the three-thirty whistles. Two of the Garramone brothers came in as well as some of the construction guys. The bar got busier.

Old Dominick would yank on the beer one tap, tipping the glass slightly; he'd fill it up. The final motion—coup de grace—was whipping the foam off the top with the whale bone, that ivory-colored piece that resembled half of a twelve-inch ruler. It would skim the rapidly rising foam off of the top of the beer glass. ("Hey, Frankie, do *ya tink* it is really from a real whale?")

Back to the Medal of Gold coffee cans. Papa Tony emptied them and counted out six dollars and fifty cents, a small ransom to working men, a lot of cold beer to some, a half week's work to most.

As was customary in those days, the eight men who had played that afternoon would play once more to see who would be the boss, and second place, the *sotto* boss. They played a form of primeer, where the sevens were valued cars (then the sixes, fives, and so on down the line—pitcher cards, other than kings—were nothing). It was a poor man's game. Royalty was neither part of their life, nor was it welcomed. The pot would give one of them absolute power. The eight men sat, four to a table, two games, but now it was cut-throat. Each was dealt four cards and a pair of sevens was almost golden. A couple of sixes was OK, too. The cards were dealt face up. Dark, sometimes squinting, eyes darted from here to there and back, and down at what was in front of the player. *"Cum ona sette . . . cum ona! Meangya . . . sie . . . oofah . . . un rei . . . un cavollo . . . eh . . . en fi nuto!"* (Squeezing for a seven . . . a couple of face cards . . . oofah . . . I'm done!).

Each table had a winner, but the holder of the best hand (table one or two) would be designated boss. The guy who "showed" was designated sotto boss; who also had power, but not total. Bull Dog won that particular afternoon.

With the seven of diamonds, seven of clubs, a five and a four, he won handsomely. He tended to be pompous and somewhat arrogant by most of the patron standards, but the cards made him boss. (Bull Dog thought that his winning was a talent or a skill; forgetting all those times that afternoon, he contributed to that particular Medal of Gold coffee can.)

The house rules were that the pot had to be spent entirely on drinks from the bar. The boss made all the selections simply because the trays were his. The sotto boss, after proper protocol—a nod or a favorable hand gesture from the boss—could take a drink and also invite others (but just one at a time) to partake of the *abondanza* of drinks. Should the boss not wish someone to have a drink, he'd quietly and discreetly cross his eyes, looking at the tip of his nose, and shake his head back and forth; sometimes a boss would just look away and ignore the sotto boss's request.

Fridone's acceptance

The Boss, like a king sitting on his throne and holding court, was omnipotent (the rules and protocol of the game of premèer were always strictly adhered to). He could delegate his sotto Boss to take the treasury and buy trays of liquid refreshment. The Boss (at this point) however, had the option to order any drinks he liked (or some of his friend's favorite drinks, maybe the partner he had played with all that afternoon). Other than the Boss's wishes, which must be obeyed, the sotto Boss . . . would then proceed to attend to the disposal of the entire Medal of Gold Coffee Can Treasury . . . as he deemed . . . fit and proper . . . just and fair.

Bull Dog leaned back in his chair, puffed on his Tuscany cigar and with a little pomp, (and loud enough for all to hear) ordered, "Una dubbla scot-cha, due Anisette and una sambucca." To the veteran players, the order seemed strange. But Bull Dog was Bull Dog and today HE was the Boss.

Joey continued to mesmerize his audience as they sat and squirmed on the concrete stoop. He told all of them, "PaPa Tony was the Sotto Boss." As the name would imply, PaPa Tony was old and respected and loved by those he knew and those he called amici or piasano. (Friend and neighbor.)

Coffee can in hand PaPa Tony went up to the bar and waited briefly for Dominic. Dominic's quick smile . . . which always made people feel just a little bit better . . . maybe because the smile was genuine . . . and he greeted the sotto Boss with a snappy, "Pronto !!!" The bartender then reached down to a shelf just beneath the bar, put two circular serving trays on the bar in front of PaPa Tony, smiled again and gave him an approving nod . . . he was ready when Papa Tony was.

Papa Tony ordered the liquor first, and Dominick, as was his well practiced style, got a shot glass out, raised it to eye level, poured a solid shot of scotch into it, shook it into a tumbler that had some ice in it, and then added the second. The remainder of the Boss's special order was poured in the same professional manner but in their own shot glasses. All were placed on one of the available trays. Old Papa Tony just watched. He was not smiling.

The old man was thinking; with a pot that big, the Boss could have all the beer or wine he wanted and there would still be a half-barrel for everyone else. Now, because of the extravagant order, the old man wasn't sure. "Eeh" he thought, "the boss might not always be right . . . but . . . by the rules . . . he was always the Boss." Dominic told him how much the liquor was and Papa Tony reached into the Medal of Gold coffee can and produced enough quarters, with two half dollar coins, to cover the obligation. He then counted what remained in the treasury, made a quick calculation if it was to be quality or quantity. He opted volume. The balance of the treasury went to glasses of beer. In the old man's mind he thought, maybe that way more men would enjoy his and Bull Dog's good fortune that warm summer evening.

As dictated by the long and complicated rules of protocol, (which were practiced so faithfully by all) the Boss and the sotto Boss sat alone at the Boss's table. The full trays properly placed in the center, and of course, within easy reach of the Boss and the sotto Boss. Other players, participants, and hopefuls, stood at the bar or remained seated at their tables. They just watched, some with half smiles, looking at one another, then at the trays . . . the beer glasses already starting to sweat on the outside. They knew that they were all just subjects to the Boss's (and in a very small part . . . good old Papa Tony's) slightest whim.

One of the trays was a Utica Club tray, the other a Coca-Cola tray, both were full and set between the two men. The pretty face of a woman painted onto the Coca-Cola tray was covered with twelve sweaty glasses of beer. Bull Dog studied how his cigar was burning by twisting back and forth between his thumb and forefinger, it met with his approval and then he flicked its gray half inch of ash onto the floor. He adjusted his eyeglasses slightly, reached over and picked up the filled scotch tumbler. He lifted it, swung around so that he could use the natural light coming from one of the side windows to examine the liquid and ice, looked around a little then took a sip. It was quiet around the Boss's table.

Finoccohio could kill a hundred Bull Dogs without even trying. *Yeah!!—dat's for sure!!!*

Little PaPa Tony, waited until the Boss had drank more than half of his double scotch and, as he was permitted to do as Sotto Boss, with an open hand, pointed to a beer on the tray, (and because he did not want to ask for himself first) asked the Boss, ""May I offer your partner Zio Rocco, a drink?' Bull Dog did not respond, instead he watched the ceiling fan spin for a few seconds, tipped and emptied his tumbler, gave an audible and satisfying "aah!!", and reached over for an anisette from the tray. No answer came to PaPa Tony's request.

A denial??? Papa Tony felt uncomfortable, withdrew his open palm, and just waited. Zio Rocco only hooded his eyes as he watched the Boss sip his new drink. Witnessing this, one of Zio Rocco's sons standing at the bar turned to his brother standing next to him and said, "*Whadda asshole!*" PaPa Tony looked at the floor where the insulted player sat, and from under his bushy and shaggy gray eyebrows tried to raise his eyes to look at, and to apologize to Zio Rocco. PaPa Tony was embarrassed and ashamed. Zio Rocco caught his eye and with a slight jog of the head, conveyed to him, it was nothing . . . and no offense taken . . . I understand your predicament.

The Boss . . . now closer to a tyrant than the participant a few minutes ago . . . finished the two remaining shots in short order. It is the sotto Boss's duty to distribute the goods. PaPa Tony wondered "what should I do, how do I handle the boss. I gotta break the ice. Nobody is talking, only the boss is enjoying himself." Then an idea came to him.

PaPa Tony leaned forward a little, gestured with his open hand again at the trays and politely asked if the Sotto Boss could have a cold beer to quench a sudden thirst. The Boss half smiled and nodded, and said. "I'll join you." Two beers came off of the Utica Club tray and, now, only one beer remained on that tray. As Papa Tony was satisfying his thirst, he wondered if his boss really didn't want to have any of the players drink from the winnings. Maybe the Boss wanted to go outside the players. It was of course his prerogative. PaPa Tony did not notice Bull Dog momentarily staring at Finoccohio. Bull Dog held him in a sort of contempt, dislike . . . thought him to be very peasant-like the crudest type, never will be an American, no fear of that . . . just a big ugly ox of a man, who disgusted him.

PaPa Tony looked around, first to the bar. He saw Zio Rocco's sons . . . aha . . . but no . . . even if the Boss would nod his approval . . . the boys would decline because of the slight to their father earlier. Once an offer was made and accepted, you could only refuse any future offer by being willing to match and pay for what ever else was left on the tray. PaPa Tony spotted Fridone, who came in with the textile crowd. He asked the Boss's permission to offer Fridone a drink; the boss nodded his approval.

Good old Fridone was at the far end of the bar, his little left foot on the bar rail, enjoying his De Nobli and talking to Finoccohio who was still seated at his table. Finoccohio, had just finished two plates of fagiolo and verdura, (beans and greens) a plate of peppers (fried in olive oil) and a loaf and a half of bread. As he poured out the last half glass of beer from his pitcher, he was telling Fridone how tasty the peppers were, and that he thought that Fridone should order some . . . with bread . . . of course, and eat . . . "You are much too skinny" said the giant of the man to his best friend. Fridone smiled sheeplessly and said it would give him "Accitta". (Acid indigestion) He was never a big eater. He heard someone call . . . "aya Fridone . . . Fridone . . ."

and turn to see that it was Papa Tony asking for his attention. Fridone smiled again and nodded to Tony and said . . . "se . . . che voglio?" (Yes . . . what do you want?) PaPa Tony answered, "'The Boss' offers you a drink from the tray . . . what do you say??"

"Eh ya perche non!! con piacere!!" (Why not? With pleasure!) Fridone walked over to the boss's table, where PaPa Tony reached over and took the last beer off of the Utica Club tray and handed it to him. Still smiling Fridone took it, tipped his head to the Boss and said "Grazia!!" "Aahh" thought Papa Tony, that's his game he doesn't want any of the contributors to drink . . . That is okay . . . they'll not die of thirst tonight . . . and will have justification to cut Bull Dog out when and if they are bosses."

Papa Tony finally felt better with his recently calculated knowledge of the Boss's wishes. He felt he could go on now and distribute the Coca-Cola tray to some of the working patrons. He quickly looked around and spotted the broad shouldered slightly balding Finoccohio. He leaned forward a bit and asked the Boss's permission to offer the big man a beer. Bull Dog was puffing his cigar and watching the blue gray smoke rise toward the ceiling fan. He did not immediately reply, PaPa Tony was about to ask him again, when he nodded quickly and as Papa Tony would later vividly recall, his smile was more of a sneer. He wondered why . . . but would not wonder for very long.

That poor dumb hard working ox of a man . . . who is he harming? . . . Why him?

Full Tray . . . Finnochio's Dilemma

Papa Tony signaled to the big man to come to the boss's table. Finnochio smiled, got up and lumbered to the table. With the same hand gesture used previously, Tony's open palm pointed to the filled Coca-Cola tray. Finnochio still smiling, jerked a quick nod to Tony and another to Bull Dog, by way of expressing his appreciation and thanks. He picked a glass from the tray and the void created by the selection revealed that the pretty girl painted on the tray was a redhead with ringlets. He started back to his table, drink in hand. Bull Dog reached over and touched Papa Tony's forearm, both leaned forward and Bull Dog whispered something into the sotto Boss's ear. Poor old Papa Tony looked confused and alarmed, shook his head no . . . but the Boss shook his head yes . . . demanding that he be obeyed. Tony sighed, took a deep breath and with a sinking, heavy heart, asked Finnochio to return to the table.

The big but gentle man returned and soon was towering over the table. Papa Tony cleared his throat, started to say something even he himself couldn't hear, and then, at a slightly higher pitch told him ". . . the boss wants you to finish the tray . . ." Tony was looking directly into Finnochio's eyes when he started, but when he finished, his head was down and he was staring at nothing.

The 'acceptance rule' now applied to Finnochio. He had willing and innocently accepted the first drink offer, now he had only one of two alternatives: obey or buy another full tray. Few, if any players, have ever seen the rule applied in such a manner; none at the volume of that filled Coca-Cola tray.

"Hey' said Finnochio, "not all of them . . . e troppo!", with a wave of his hand he continued, "look at all the others . . . let them enjoy too!!" Finnochio really believed that they were kidding . . . sta cherzo . . . but when he looked at Papa Tony . . . who remained staring shamefully at the floor . . . and then looked up to see Bull Dog looking straight at him . . . smirking . . . did the reality of the situation become apparent to him.

Only the Boss, and the letch Riccocha, . . . (who paraded his mistress in front of his children and saintly wife and taking her to the bedroom and closing the door) . . . only those two found it amusing. The others who could hear and see what was going on, became very quiet and pensive. Many of them thought, "Whadda jerk!!! He lets everybody go dry . . . Except for old Tony and Frirdone . . . and he sticks that poor working slob with a loaded tray . . . whadda friggin asshole . . . he used his buddy Firdone to set him up . . . how could Finnochio see it coming??? Whadda prick!!"

Finnochio looked at Bull Dog with a incredulous open mouth stare . . . "perche . . . ???" The Boss in a silent reply, only gestured to the Coca-Cola tray as Tony had done earlier and continued smirking. The big man remained in a state of semi shock . . . his brain reeling. How can I drink all that now?? After paying for his dinner earlier, he only had a quarter in his pocket. "Maybe I could ask Fridone for a dollar or something . . . How much is that tray??? Dollar?? Dollar and half??"

Bull Dog seems to enjoy Finnochio's dilemma and just sat there watching him and puffing on his cigar. The blue-gray smoke was being pulled upward by the humming ceiling fan. The Boss thought to himself, "Look at that big oaf . . . a real hick farmer . . . campagna—el—io . . . they don't come too much dumber than him . . . a piece of junk . . . like his little mousey buddy Fridone . . . he too probably signs his name with an . . . X." You always have trouble with guys like him in November when you gotta get them to vote the "'right' way."

Bull Dog was ornery . . . maybe not always this ornery . . . but ornery. It was not only his looks . . . those flabby jowls . . . flush cheeks . . . eyeglasses that seemed pressed into his face . . . a thick neck . . . that gave him his descriptive nick name, it was his attitude, his disposition and his arrogance. Today, maybe it was the heat that contributed to the high level spitefulness . . . or the lack of sleep from the night before . . . or his wife never ending nagging for a 'totally new electric refrigerator' . . . or his fatherly obligation to marry off three un-attractive daughters . . . or his two sons who worked on the rail road and insisted on keeping half of their pay envelope . . . or . . . or . . . whatever. He stared at Finnochio and simply thought . . . "Let the big bastard twist in the wind. He was just a piece of junk anyway!!!" The smirk, like his cigar never left his face.

The Pig Could Do It

The kids on the rear stoop could almost smell the beer and the aroma of the peppers frying in the kitchen in anticipation of what was to come—gasping, holding their breath; some could almost see the beads of sweat forming on Finnochio's upper lip. Others thought they could see him looking around in a panic, disoriented manner, looking dumbfounded and confused—all that beer!—alone, no help, no family, snookered and knowing it. There was a smirk on a face—the face that was looking at him.

"He would do it . . . he had to . . ."

Still standing at the boss's table, he retrieved his second glass of beer and downed it. The void created by the withdrawal of the glass from the tray revealed that the pretty Coca-Cola girl had greenish eyes and a perfectly shaped left eyebrow. And so it went—the third, the fourth the fifth. Each time he finished one, he made certain that h would not place the empty back into the tray. The big man wanted to deliberately clutter the table. It was only Papa Tony, whose downward-looking eyes watched the painted pretty girl blossom . . . like a flower . . . on the bottom of the wet Coca-Cola tray.

Between the ninth and tenth beer, Fridone, who was helplessly watching, went to Finnochio and beg him to at least sit down at a nearby table, kiddingly reminding him that if he fell who would be able to pick him up. With an angry shake of the head, he refused. His brain was starting to get foggy; he would soon be burping and trying to suppress an eruption building deep in his stomach. "How many were left on the tray?"

"Only two . . ."

"I'll show this smirking bastard how to drink beer."

In a little less than twenty-five minutes, he had the last glass in his hand. Papa Tony, until he died, never forgot each and every detail of the girl's pretty face painted on the now-empty Coca-Cola tray. Not once did he raise his eyes from the tray. In the years to come, he still felt a tang of shame when he thought about his part—innocent as it was—in this affair. The boss was no longer smirking; and when the last glass was empty, he was no longer the boss—the game was over.

Finnochio, who was still standing at Bull Dog's table, choked down a burp by clenching his teeth for a moment (until the urge passed), gave his antagonist a quick jerky nod, and stepped away. "There! I did it." On the way to his table he stumbled a bit but didn't lose his balance, flopped into his chair, and reached for the towelette/moppean. He wanted to wipe his face and feel the coolness of the damp cloth. Fridone quickly came to his side, pulled up the other chair, and in a half whisper asked if he was all right. The big man nodded yes and smiled weakly. Fridone, too, nodded, saying, "Good! Okay! Me too! Good!" Finnochio could kill a hundred bulldogs. Yeah, with one hand tied behind his back. Yeah, he could do it without even trying. Yeah, look at how big he is. He works in the foundry, carries tons of iron all day, and got all kinds of big muscles—the biggest. He could if he wants too! Yeah . . .

At this point in this adventure, the former boss made a mistake that he would regret for the remainder of his long life. His disdain for the large man did not diminish one iota, and leaning back in his chair he said loudly, "I figured the pig could drink them all."

"I figured the pig could drink them all."

Those words, "I figured the pig could drink them all," slowly penetrated the fog of Finnochio's brain. He did no immediately understand the meaning—nor the intended recipient—because he was again trying to suppress another burp. Such an accident, if heard by all, could be interpreted as a sign of weakness by his peers. But then certain words did emerge from the fog in his brain and became a little more coherent: "Drink them all . . . pig . . . I figured the pig could . . ."

"Who is saying that? Who is he saying it to? Why is he saying, 'I figured the pig . . . drink them all . . .' What is he talking about?"

Finnochio shook his head—like they say—to clear the cobwebs. He shook his head again, and then Fridone was the first to see it coming, and it frightened him. The facial muscles that cause one to squint seem to relax; a look of understanding and revelation showed, and in a few heartbeats his eyes widened, his nostrils flared, his teeth clicked and then his mouth opened very wide to release a savage scream. Little Fridone reached for and touched his forearm, and in a desperate plea said, *"No . . . no . . . lasciare . . . per la amore de Dio . . . non!"* (No, no let it go . . . for the love of God . . . don't!)

Tony hung on every word uttered from Joey's mouth, unblinking, mouth open, scared. He involuntarily found himself forcing his sphincter to shut and shift his weight from one buttock to the other on the cool concrete stoop. Finnochio could pulverize a hundred bulldogs! Yeah, pulverize him to dust!

The Fight . . . The Stop Sign

Then Joey said Finnocchio left his chair. Joey thought he was airborne—his big arms over his head like a King Kong screaming at the top of his lungs, charging like a wounded and angry rhino. Bull Dog's mouth dropped open, his eyes widened and filled with fear, his cigar fell on the table between the twelve empty beer glasses and by the Coca-Cola tray with the pretty redhead still smiling at the ceiling, the blood drained from Bull Dog's face.

Joey said Finnocchio increased in size—twice, no *three* times; the room vibrated under his fierce charge. Joey said he increased three times intending it to be literally—not figuratively. No need—his audience took it figuratively because in their mind's eye, they saw it too!

Papa Tony saw all those glasses and the pretty tray girl go flying off of the table, some upward, others sideways; the table legs just missed his face by inches. A blur of a large object flashed past his face and then the clashing sound of all that glass breaking and the table slamming on the floor. The uproar was the loudest old Papa Tony ever heard, and it seemed to resonate everywhere. Some of the men at the bar were yelling; others remained open mouthed, staring in disbelief—frozen: *How could a man as big as that move that fast; did he clear two tables on that dive?* Poor Little Fridone was screaming for Finnocchio to stop; his next breath was pleading for others to stop him.

A split-second there was Bull Dog's shoes, ankles, trousers, legs, all at Papa Tony's eye level from his still-seated position at the boss's table. Bull Dog's back, shoulders, his head, the back of his neck all seemed to hit and bounce off the floor at the same instant; his legs and heels following a second after. His eyeglasses hung askew on the left side of his face and only remained there because the eyeglasses' frame's left ear hook stubbornly held.

He felt the weight of each one of his past sins: every impure thought, every curse word he ever uttered, every unjustified insult—all that—squarely and heavily pressing on his chest. Something large and strong tightened around his neck; he opened his eyes and could only see Finnocchio's ugly angry red face—eyes as big as coffee cup saucers, surreal and grotesque; this has got to be what the devil looks like. "*Santa Maria auito a mei* (Saint Mary help me; I'm in hell.) I am in hell . . . in hell . . . Someone, please help . . . dear God, please . . . I can't breathe . . . please . . . God . . . help!"

No one man pulled off Bull Dog's attacker; no one man could; it was a combined effort of six to eight, at times ten men. Still another table was tipped over; some of the rescuers were pushed, shoved, and some even thrown away by the furious giant. They would nonetheless scramble quickly to their feet, oblivious to the broken glass all around (some suffering minor cuts), and charge back into the fray, determined to prevent what was sure to be a barehanded murder.

Fridone in a frantic state tried several times to get close to the big man, only to be tossed away (unfortunately) further than the other rescuers, but he kept coming back, finally getting close enough to his ear and yelling over the surrounding commotion, "Basta . . . basta . . . laciere . . . basta . . . per l'amore de Dio lacarier . . . basta! (Enough . . . enough . . . let him go . . . Enough for the love of God!)"

Fridone had one hand on Finnochio's left ear near his cheek, the other on his right biceps, pulling; all three of them sprawled on the oft beer-splashed floor with that distinct old beer odor. Then Fridone sensed an infinitesimal and minute change, like a taunt spring slowly returning to a state of rest; Little Fridone from his fingertips dug deeply into his friend's arm, sensed the hatred and rage and the shame, the embarrassing insult, and humiliation ebbing and falling away into an abyss.

Finnocchio first shouted and then gradually whispering and kept repeating, "I am not a pig . . . I am not a pig . . . I am working man . . . I love my God . . . I am not a pig!".

A long forgotten scene from his childhood flashed across his mind . . . clear . . . as if it happened just yesterday. He and his mother, with buckets of swill went out to feed the landlord's pigs . . . "*il patrone*," the Boss's. He remembered how the pigs smelled, how they would almost kill one another trying to get to the swill that he was dumping into the trough; in that muddy sty. He was always careful when doing that, he was there once when in a feeding frenzy a pig snapped and nipped his mother's leg. The wound drew blood . . . red . . . it had stained her long black skirt . . . and to this day he still felt a hurt . . . as if it were he who was bitten by the lousy . . . "animale . . . bastardo . . . animale . . . selvaggio." A soulless being. Never washing before eating . . . never thanking God for his food.

Like Faulkner's small dog in "The Bear" . . . they have already determined, "I do not have an immortal soul . . ." Animale squealing and snapping and shoving to get a bit of what (??) . . . nothing. "I am not a pig!! I am a lot of things, but I am not a pig!! I am stupid . . . I can not read good . . . I am a fool . . . people laugh at me when I don't understand why . . . but . . . but . . . dear God in heaven . . . Blessed Mother . . . I am not a pig!!!"

A lot of this Finnocchio said aloud . . . low and subdued . . . only his friend Fridone, who remained sitting on the floor beside him, could hear. The smaller man gently reached one arm and hand around the big man's neck . . . the other hand cupping that massive jaw . . . tried to gently rock him . . . and just repeated, simple . . ." . . . . Lo so . . . I know . . . lo so . . . I know . . . lo so." Fridone did not rock Finnocchio . . . it was more like he was just gently bouncing off of him.

And that broken giant of a man continued his remorseful litany . . . I try to wash my hands before I eat or break a piece of bread . . . I do not speak until I am asked . . . I do not bother others . . . I am not a pig . . . I do not wish others the mal-occhio . . . I want to be accepted . . . not even loved . . . just accepted . . . I am not a pig!!" The small man swayed and rocked to his feet first, and what in could have been interpreted as a sign of helpful assistance and aid, it appeared as if he helped the big man to his feet . . . but not really. Finnochio stood when he wanted to, sat when he wanted to, and lay down when he wanted to.

The two lonely bachelors stood, the big one steadied himself a little, the smaller one appeared to be reaching as if he could keep that mountain of a man from falling, and looked around. The barroom was a mess. Dominick and a few of the bar patrons were attending to Bull Dog . . .

mainly to see if he was still alive . . . still breathing. Old Papa Tony . . . who was eventually knocked off of his seat at the Boss's table at some time in the confrontation . . . got up . . . re-set his chair . . . sat in it again . . . and looked around in total amazement and bewilderment ". . . **WOW**.!!! how strong is that man ??? What would it take to . . . harness . . . contain . . . corral . . . him?? Non so!! (I don't know.) I am much too old for this !!!"

Zio Rocco Garromone's elder sons came to his immediate assistance. It wasn't needed . . . , as close as he was to the melee . . . the only "action" he saw was when he lifted his foot to and stopped the Coca-Cola tray from sliding across the room. The old man with seven sons who all had at least one son of their own . . . the first always named Rocco, smiled inwardly and said, "That bastard had it coming to him."

In the old neighborhood, Catherine and Jay streets ran east and west, Kossuth and Pellettieri ran north and south. Most city blocks are rectangular, of course, and in this case Catherine and Jay, are the . . . what is it ??? . . . the elongated side of the rectangular. The two came out of Goomba Joe's Restaurant, under the humming ceiling fan, through the often slamming screen door, down the first step, then down the stoop step . . . on to Jay Street. Less than five paces for Finnocchio . . . seven for Fridone . . . they turned left and headed north on Pellettieri Avenue. Fridone was taking the big guy back to their boarding house on Broad Street. Wasn't far . . . block . . . block and a half to Zio Pasquale's boarding house.

The trek going north on Pelletteri took you past an alley way, a three decker frame building that belonged to Pasquale Durante (and eventually to his daughter and son-in-law Vic the Barber) . . . past Don Vincenzo (another Sicilian) who had a barn-garage (just behind his small one story and a half frame house) where they made boot-leg liquor in the old days. Young Tony's Uncle Mike once had to jump from the roof of that barn . . . and . . . seek asylum . . . in the dead of night . . . at his younger sister's home . . . with six kids . . . five girls . . . only one boy . . . her husband . . . and the story goes . . . he hid under the kid's bed. Uncle Sarafino was a hard working man that laid new tile in private bathrooms and restaurants and in rest-rooms . . . only trying to live their lives . . . as they saw fit . . . AND . . . as best as they could . . . in those tough times.

A couple of weaving steps . . . a short distance . . . then . . . the John Blaze Building . . . still another three story brownstone (six families),the unique feature of this brownstone structure was the corner angular stone placed above the third story flat . . . directly at the juncture of Catherine and Pelletieri Avenue . . . it proudly read . . . "Blaze 1904." Like the Perretta building on Jay St. and Kossuth avenue.

On those warm summer evening . . . if you listen closely . . . you could hear the voices of young children singing the cadence of . . ." . . . my mother gave me a nickel to buy a . . ." The 'sing-song' music drifted down the street.

They crossed Catherine Street and walked past the empty but fenced—in corner lot. The lot was owned by the Marraffa family as was the three store frame structure which abutted it. The Marraffa occupied the entire first floor, and there were four apartments, two on each level. It was one of the very few structures with a pitched roof/attic above the third story. Mr. Marraffa was a carpenter.

They slowly walked and wobbled by and passed the old bakery. Sometimes in the early hours of still another work day morning (when the textile mills' screeching steam whistle blew) a person could smell the bread baking. (Who doesn't like the smell of bread baking???)

The whistle blew at six AM . . . six forty-five . . . six fifty-five . . . and . . . then . . . seven . . . straight up.

The kitchen clock, in the shape of the downtown main library, the church bells from St. Anthony and other parishes announcing ten minutes before the Padre and the altar boys left the sanctuary to say the next mass . . .

(Ad Diem que litificato il mei junventdu tium . . . I will go to the altar of God . . . to God the joy of my youth) . . . that Waltham or Boliva wrist watch you got for confirmation . . . all those and all others . . . were not official. There was always room for error . . . but not those mill whistles . . . no-sir-ree . . . never wrong!

"They" . . . whoever really owned the mills and gave out yellow pay envelopes (cash) to the workers . . . many with cotton lint still matted in their hair . . . allowed . . . maybe as a community service . . . the whistle too loudly and joyful screech in every New Year's Day. "Watch the clock . . . What's it say?? . . . eleven fifty six . . . somebody open the door or a window . . . we don't want to miss them!!! The screech . . . Happy New Year!! Hugging and kissing . . . somebody shooting a shotgun . . . maybe a German Luger (a war souvenir) . . . somewhere in the back yards or alleys.

Is it the Brits from London who say you are a Cockney only if you were born within the sound of Bows Bells??? . . . or something like that. In the old neighborhood, New Year's eve was referred to as the Whistles. A life time later, some would still say . . . . ". . . Whadda ya doin for the Whistles . . ."

Fridone and Finnocchio were not too far away from the boarding house now, only a half of a block. Just pass the fence of the Utica Sheets Mills. This fence . . . was a barrier . . . it ran (and overlapped slightly) from the furthest northeast corner of the bakery's property . . . straight as an arrow . . . to the nearest northeast corner of the Ritrona property, with its yellow two story frame structure. In the center of the fence was a yellow and black octangular city stop sign. The sign's eight sides were stripped in a black three-quarter inch border and the word STOP yelled at you from dead center. The remainder/background was a bright yellow. The word stop had circular glass balls in it that acted as reflectors when head lights fell upon them at night. There were twenty-eight such reflector orbs . . . funny how you remember something like that.

The fence . . . and . . . the sign . . . proclaimed to man & beast alike, this part of Pellettieri Avenue was a Dead End. An official City Stop Sign . . . a deterrent . . . a barrier . . . to all your unspoken and secret dreams.

The larger man first . . . , followed by the smaller . . . walking sideways, toes twisted out . . . to the east and to west . . . side stepped . . . heels touch . . . side step again . . . stepping . . . squeezing into and by . . . that waist high wooden posted and metal meshed fence that the textile mill erected. (There was about a 10 inch space between the bakery outside wall & the second to last fence post. That was the width; the length was about four feet. The fence was there to stop vehicular traffic (which it did) and discouraging pedestrian traffic (which it did not.)

The mills owned that big vacant lot facing Broad St. A very large lot . . . Enough to support two large-double billboards on either end, one that was for west bound traffic to read and the other was for east bound traffic traveling Broad Street; route 5S through Utica. Finnocchio had been biting his lips since he left the bar and shaking his head every so often trying to erase the words . . .

". . . I figured the pig could do it . . ." They were walking slowly past the green billboard on the west side of the mill's lot, when he slowed his pace and eventually came to a complete stop. He steadied himself with his left arm against the billboard and broke down and wept aloud. Fridone stopped too, reached out and touched his friend's shoulder and just said '. . . lo so . . . I know . . . lo so . . . I know . . ." well before Finnocchio said aloud, between his sobs . . . "I am not a pig . . . am not a . . ."

If you listen closely, you could still hear from far away . . ." . . . My mother gave me a nickel to buy a pickle . . . I didn't buy a pickle I bought some chewing gum . . . Ya da da da chewing gum ya da da chewing gum . . ."

The next morning, both were awaken by the six o'clock whistle. Zio Pasquale's boarding house was just across street from a large and very long brick four story textile mill. Soon, they would both leave . . . Fridone to one of the mills . . . Finnocchio to the foundry.

On the work day mornings, it was only the large man who walked sideways . . . heel touching the each other and the side stepping . . . squeezing into . . . and by . . . the waist high fence to go to work. The fence that told the world to STOP and that Pelletieri Ave was a dead end. But . . . sometimes you had to walk sideways just a little to get ahead . . . just a little.

In the quiet of his screened patio Tony mused . . .". yeah !! . . . come to think of it . . . it was a stop sign and NOT a dead end sign . . . wonder why that was??? Ah . . .

maybe that's the way the mills wanted it . . . maybe the city ran out of Dead End signs . . ." He wasn't sure of the reason . . . but he was sure as shooting that there were twenty-eight round reflectors in the word STOP. He remembered counting them. He sipped some more red wine. There is no such thing as bad wine . . . there is wine and there is vinegar. He thought of all those men from his past . . . their dreams their hopes their lives . . . it didn't make him sad . . . nor happy . . . nor glad, nor angry.

Tony looked deep into the purple half-filled wine bottle. He squinted and concentrated, still no change: . . . no sadness . . . no happiness . . . no joy . . . no anger. There is no such thing as bad wine; there is wine and there is vinegar.

His wife was right . . . he drinks too much in his old age.

The Neighborhood

Turk The Lebanese . . . . The PFC Club
Starry night . . . E-Mail
Dentist . . . Chicken Store
Wine Making
The Clothes Line . . . The Brownstone
The Scissors . . . Fresh fish
Porch versus Stoop
Cigars and Fingers

Turk-The Lebanese . . . The PFC Club

Tony would often visit his aging mother on a monthly basis, sometimes twice a month. She had been widowed since 1955. He would stay on Friday and Saturday and then would return home on Sunday afternoons. He'd meet his older brother for breakfast at least one of those weekend mornings. They would always have breakfast at a very popular diner on the fringe of the old neighborhood, by "new" Proctor Park. The diner was run by a grandson of an old and dear friend of Tony's family. His grandparents have long since passed on, and those who knew them would always remember them with the greatest respect and highest esteem. They were, beyond the shadow of doubt, the salt of the good earth.

The diner's clientele were mostly contemporaries of Tony and his brother's generation; naturally he had the postmen and deliverymen and runners from nearby construction sites with huge, huge orders to go. It was a very successful operation (*benedica*), so much so that they would only serve breakfast and lunch, closing the doors at 3:00 PM. Fridays, one could get a fish fry up until 6:00 PM. But only Fridays! The working people came in and out; Tony, his brother, and their contemporaries would linger in the booths, order extra coffee, teasing the waitress, and going back in time and talking mostly about the "old days."

On one such extended breakfast, Tony was delighted to run into an old high school classmate, Fran "the Turk" Joseph. They called him Turk because he wasn't Italian (he was Lebanese) or because of his very ruddy complexion, but either way, the Turk was always one of the guys. Tony remembered that he didn't have a mean bone in his body and could run like a deer.

It was Turk who told Tony about the Proctor Fifties Club (their old high school—Proctor) and its growing popularity: it was always better than the previous years, starting way back in 1994 and going stronger. "You gotta come to at least one of the suppers . . . third Tuesday of every month."

Tony replied, "Yeah . . . maybe . . . someday when I'm in town." His inner thoughts were *The middle of the week . . . kinda long drive . . . Yeah, maybe someday, it sounds good.* "You gotta come, Tony! . . . You gotta come . . . It's great!" Good old Turk, not a mean bone in his body.

Growing up, he was a fat kid with curly hair and until he was five-ish, his mother never had his hair cut. At about that time, and for many years to come, the Italian-American branch of my mother's family was very close. The eldest uncle, because he came to America in 1905 and because his father was denied entry into the United States at Ellis Island in 1913, became the patriarch of the family. The family was indeed close, not only spiritually but physically. The three sisters with two brothers all lived within a block-and-a-half radius: there on Catherine Street with two on Pelletieri Avenue. Their children all grew up together in their age clichés and strata. It was simple, and it was effective, and it was in total harmony with the universe and the way things should be and were.

When Tony retired, he purchased a new pickup truck, forest green. He loved it and still does. The pickup truck was something he always secretly wanted, like a red wagon when he was a kid, with silver hub cabs, varnished side racks, thick rubber tires, a black pulling handle and its own rubber grip, making one believe that his hands would never hurt because of the grip. But this truck was a beauty!

As time went by, he would in total honesty tell his family, "You know *sumptin*? Sometime you wish for *sumptin*'... and after you get it... the newness... the wonder... the shine wears off? Ya know *whadda* I mean? The thrill wears off and you are half disappointed that it wasn't cracked up to what you thought it would be? Ya know *whadda* I mean? Well let me tell ya guy... It was better than what I hoped it would be!"

Tony's grandkids not only named his beloved truck the Big Green Machine but insisted on playing on it (the bed) and playing in it (the cabin). The machine had taken Tony more than two hundred thousand miles. On its many trips home to East Utica and the PFC club meeting, it was unflinching, joyful, running full bore, charging north and home. There was a sense of urgency for both driver and machine (if it had a soul)—Ya gotta get *dare*! Ya gotta! "Will it be *dare* tomorrow? Or the day after? How long is it *gunna* be around? How long are ya gonna be 'round?"

Because death is right there over your left shoulder, behind your ear—look! Shit. He's gone; you caught just a glimpse of his shadow... you gotta charge back to a time and place that was yesterday... to those... if they are still alive... who remember and know... He is still there waiting for you to drop into an abyss... twisting and falling... screaming silently... falling... twisting...

like an old rotting telephone pole swaying in the cold November sunshine.

"Hail Mary full of grace, the Lord is with thee . . ."

Falling . . . twisting . . . downward . . . I really wanna be good! Help me!

Ah! Here's the Clark Summit's toll booth . . . How much? Sorry it is the smallest I got.

Starry Night . . . E-Mail

Page Down

One of Tony's first thoughts that morning was of Joey. He slipped his foot into one of his old blue slippers (always the right one first . . . a creature of habit), stepped into the other and started to walk. He felt something on and in the left slipper . . . "what the hell?? How did that get in there?" A small piece of rice gravel, he must have dragged it into the house somehow from yesterday's concrete project. He was making a new base for the birdbath, well anyway, that's what it looked like after he had taken it out of the slipper and examined it more closely.

And then . . . you know how your mind works sometime??? . . . as he looked at his bare foot . . . his ugly hammer toes . . . it triggered a mental image from years and years ago . . . he remembered . . . the old stout Italian ladies following the statues of Sts. Cosmo & Damiano in the late Sunday morning procession down Catherine Street. Barefooted, their lips appeared to be trembling, but you knew they were only praying the Rosary: some with tears streaming down their faces.

One memory triggers another, then another . . . then still another . . . he thought of Joey. Joe, Tony's God parent's eldest son, who quit high school in his third or fourth year and got a job driving a cement mixer. Drove it for more than forty years, and was very good at it, one of the best, him and, Petey-Half Man.

Tony remembered the very first monthly meeting/ dinner of the PFC Club (Proctor's Fifties Club) that he attended; Joey D'Amore was one of the first guys he ran into. The party/meeting that eventually ended up in the vacant rear parking lot of the restaurant (which saw the demise of Tony's grappa bottle and half of Pierre's Napoleon brandy bottle) turned into a very memorable evening for Tony.

Standing around the green pick-up truck, listening to one story . . . this recollection . . . that perception, one after another . . . the night was and became magic. Not a cloud in the heavens of a star filled sky . . . drinking . . . and sharing . . . from the same stolen restaurant coffee mug . . . the grappa hand—carried by Tony from one of his trips to Italy. Joey, whose mother came from the same village as Tony's father did, reminisced about growing up.

He remembered as did Tony, their mothers making 'eiricktelli' . . . home made macaroni . . . and serving it with a thick rich sauce and ricotta forte (a strong goat milk cheese). Some of the kids in the neighborhood had trouble pronouncing 'eiricktelli', and the street name was priest hats or ears. Tony and Joey both nodded enthusiastically as one reminded the other of the days that were and continued their one-up-man-ship of their history.

Joey said during the course of the evening, his mother's hands would fly when she'd make the 'eiricktella'. And Tony reminded those standing around the truck and were listening, the entire apron . . . bib included . . . was always worn when making the macaroni. He told them, 'It was not only necessary, but vital because it made the macaroni taste better!!!'

Someone else added, "Yeah !! And we didn't call it pasta . . . we called it 'macaroon' or macaroni." They agreed; wasn't it strange those two words went from English back to Italian in daily usage in just three generations?"

At a certain point . . . and Tony doesn't remember exactly when . . . on that starry and magical night . . . the 'boys' started to talk about the feasts and the processions on Sundays. Tony asked if anybody remembered the old ladies that followed the saints, and Joey replied, "Yeah!! And they were barefooted!!"

It is funny, Tony thought, as often as he recalls that incident; his sharpest recollection was how Joey's eyebrows arched up into his forehead as he nodded vigorously to emphasis the point. "Yeah", said Tony, "yeah! You're right!!! Ya'betcha ass I remember!!!"

In late May or early June of that year, Tony got an e-mail from a mutual acquaintance, telling him Joey had died. 'Bummer' was his first reaction. He had only met Joey's wife once and did not feel that comfortable expressing his condolences to her. "Louie . . . Joey's younger brother . . . where'd he live?? Canada??" He had heard Montreal. Louie was only about two years younger than we were, "our generation . . . he'd understand my feeling . . . Yeah . . . I'll write him."

Subject: . . . My condolences . . . and some shared
thoughts . . . Luigi . . . it is with genuine sadness and a kind
of melancholy disappointment that I heard the news of your
brother's passing . . . my thoughts and recollections of him
are all good . . . from the time we skipped school and went
to Syracuse North High School in his '36 Plymouth . . .
to a time before that when he showed me his lathe in the
basement of the Lansing Street homestead . . . (I remember
as if it were yesterday the look of contentment on his face as
he fingered the piece he had in the lathe for smoothness) . . .
and a very special time when he & I went up to his pigeon
coop over your father's garage . . . he picked up a pure white
pigeon . . . holding the wings with his thumb & fingers . . .
the bird's neck and head protruding out of the web of his
hand . . . . And then Joe reached back . . . like an outfielder
trying to keep the runner from taking an extra base . . .
threw the white bird into the pale blue sky . . . . It traveled
maybe ten . . . Fifteen feet . . . and then the bird spread
it wings and flew off . . . It was probably one of the most
religious scene's I've ever experienced . . . . And then . . .
there was fifty years of his life . . . And my life . . . Separate
and apart . . . We re-opened our friendship recently via the
PFC club . . . (Proctors Fifties Club) . . . It was good . . . I
guess it may have been last October or November I went
to Utica for Fran Fiorentino's art exhibit . . . Spent most
of the day with Joe . . . We met at the Florentine Cafe . . .
He did the driving . . . He took me to his home . . . and
he showed me his garage . . . and his wood working
projects . . . He said he liked making sawdust . . . to me
he made works of art . . . He was good with his hands . . .
From caressing sanded wood to holding a fragile bird . . .
I'm gonna miss 'em.

Page Up

The Saints from St. Anthony's Church always turned left off of Catherine St. onto Kossuth Ave. because west of Kossuth (800 Block of Catherine) belonged to our Lady of Mount Carmel Church.

. . . . Midway down the 900 block of Catherine . . . Standing by the curb . . . late September (Circa '43, maybe '44) . . . watching the procession of Saints Cosmo & Damiano . . . "**LOOK !!!**" old ladies carrying their shoes and clutching their Rosaries . . . following the Blessed statues . . ." Did they walk all the way from St. Anthony's??? The unforgiving Catherine Street tarmac/pavement has long since shredded their hosiery . . . what started that morning as protection between shoe and feet . . . are now just rags . . . and with each step . . . they flap over the tops of their toes. The remaining hosiery clung to their swollen ankles and wrinkled at their calves. "They are barefooted . . . barefooted!!! Must hurt!!" You can see small piece of rice gravel . . . even tiny pieces of broken glass on the street and by the curbs.

There are five of these stout weeping Italian women, limping and wobbling in their Sunday's best. ("How do you know it is their Sunday's best??? . . . Because they are wearing hats.)

A little boy tugs at his mother's dress and asks, "Why don't they wear their shoes??? "His mother bends over slightly and whispers (as if they were in church) her answer into the boy's ear," . . . "la Guerra . . ."

Dentist . . . Chicken Store

Not too long ago, Tony was having some work done on his teeth. His dentist was a good guy, maybe a year or two older than him. He was getting ready to retire, and he was going to turn over his customers (or is it a practice in dentistry?) to his son. Anyway, the old man liked to futch around in his garden and orchard; and more times than not, the conversation between him and Tony would go that way. The dentist gave Tony two of the sweetest apples he had ever eaten. Tony reciprocated by giving him a bag of figs. They kind of got to become gardening "buddies."

On one particular visit, the good doctor was in there, drilling deep and steady and long. Tony smelled something familiar, very familiar; and it brought him very far back. When the dentist finally asked him to rinse, he readily accepted that little paper cup of water with a mental weighed base, took a sip, swished it, felt the gritty stuff in his mouth, and spat it out into the circular basin the had a slow, steady stream of water circulating it. The action reminded Tony of flushing the toilet. Tony put the empty cup back. He watched the cup automatically refill with fresh water. He wiped his mouth with one of those flimsy bibs the dentist's office used and wondered, again how much weight it took to depress the spring to activate the flow of fresh water. (An eighth of a pound? Yeah, a couple of ounces maybe.)

He then said to the dentist, "You know *sumptin'*, Doc? When I was a kid, we'd buy fresh killed chickens from a chicken store in our neighborhood. When we got the bird home, my mother would unwrap it, turn on one of the gas jets on our old stove, grab one of the that poor chicken's legs with one hand and with the other take hold of what was left of the bird's neck, and kind of slowly swing back and forth over the lit gas jet. She used to come pretty close to the ring of flames, close enough to singe some of those tiny hair-like feather ends. You know what I mean, Doc?" The dentist nodded yes, and Tony could sense a smile starting to form on his lips. "It was kind of like a ritual to thoroughly cleanse the bird before she dumped it into the boiling kettle of water," Tony explained. The full smile then came on to the doctor's face, and he told Tony his mother used to do the same thing. *Whadda guy,* Tony thought. *You gotta love him . . . From my generation!*

"You know, Doc," Tony continued, "when you were drilling just now, I got a whiff of what you were drilling, and you know what, the odor reminded me of when my mother purified the chickens over the old gas jets. It smelled just like it!"

"It is the protein you smelled."

"*Hadda* ya like *dat*? Protein!" Tony said and thought, *Betcha Patsy the Chicken Man didn't know that!* And as if his subconscious raised the ante, it told him, *Betcha his grandson knew that!* (You see, Pasty the Chicken Man's grandson Pat De Carlo eventually became a dentist, too.) *Hmmm,* Tony mused, *wonder if Pat had any kids and they too became dentists, that would make old Patsy happy . . . aw anything would make that old guy happy; if his great-grandson ran his own chicken store or became an architect or a lawyer, it would not have mattered to old Patsy*

It turned from a chicken store to a hygienically and ultra-copacetic disinfected dentist's office, all in three generations. ("*Witch* one ya *tink* smelled better?") At that, Tony remembered the old days in the neighborhood.

"Donnette!" Zia Grazia called from the balcony down into the alley. "*Venga qua* (Come here)!" The girl immediately stopped her rope skipping, and even as she started heading for the staircase, she was braiding her precious skip rope. She moved toward the rear stoop and up the rear staircase. A cloud of apprehension crossed her face; that full beautiful smile left her face; and she started to worry if she had forgotten something. What? Up the staircase, all sixteen steps, around the banister to the screen door (also yellow). She remembered to reach back with her right hand to keep the screen from slamming. *You don't wanna make Ma mad,* she thought.

"Yeah, mom, *whadda* ya want?"

Zia Grazia told her that she and her two sisters and her sister-in-law Grace stopped at Patsy the Chicken Man yesterday morning (Friday). They all stopped at his store on the way home from the seven o'clock Mass (am). Yesterday was the first Friday of the month, and if one receives Holy Communion nine consecutive first Fridays, he would go to heaven upon his death. Who doesn't want to go to heaven?

The four matriarchs all ordered chickens for Sunday dinner and Monday's soups. A relieved Antoinette (she did not forget anything) was told to go and round up some of her older female cousins (Frances and Teresa from Zia Lucia's kids, Rosie and Frances from Zia Grazia's kids) and to bring along Little Tony. Maybe the little guy could help share the load.

The chickens were all paid for. She (Antoinette) was reminded to make sure Patsy didn't forget to wrap the liver, the stomach, and heart for each chicken.

"Get the girls. Get Tony and go. When you get the *gallini* (chickens), come straight home, Capirce?"

"Okay, Ma!" She left her jump rope in her bedroom by her pillow and ran out of the flat. The screen door slammed behind her. Zia Grazia cursed.

With Tony in hand, she went to Zia Lucia's. Frances and Teresa saw Young Tony and asked their mother if they too could bring their Anthony. (Their grandfather's name was Anthony.) Permission was granted. The five of them then went to get Rosie and Frances at the flat of Aunt Grace the American. Seeing the two Tony's and the flock of five older girls (mostly teenagers), Aunt Grace the American told her daughters to take young Joey along.

Their grandmother's name, in the Old Country, was really Anna Francesica; but she preferred to be called Francesca. She died in December of 1917. Their grandfather, Antonio, was away, working in the fields of Puglia, harvesting winter grain for the war when his wife passed on. Her passing and his absence had deeply saddened him until the day he himself died. When his mother would tell him that story, Young Tony could not help but notice his ma's sad eyes would become watery (each time).

A parade of five girls and three young boys marched to Patsy the Chicken Store. One of the boys had a cold, and his sister constantly reminded him to blow his nose. One of the boys had a broken shoelace; it had to be repaired by tying the ends later. The other had a big hole in his right stocking at the heel. The kids used to call that specific hole and its location a potato. This one was a big potato!

Patsy the Chicken Man was on Jay Street. Actually, it was a freestanding building in the rear of Patsy De Carlo's two-story frame house. Back in the "older" days, some of the older homes had small horse barns in the rear. Patsy converted his into his chicken store. There were four chicken stores in a two-block area, and none of them smelled too good. The converted barn was ideal—ample room to stack the wooden crates that brought the live chickens in.

The chicken crates had a door at the top and in the center, about a foot square. Sometimes a customer would look into the chicken crate, point to a fat one, and say, "*Quello!*" Patsy would reach into the crate from the square-door opening, snatch the squawking chicken by the neck or a foot or a wing—it didn't really matter where, as the animal was not long for this world. Patsy had three or four large funnel-like zinc containers tapered to a two-inch opening at the bottom. The funnels hung over a four-foot trough. That squawking bird would go into the funnel head first. The little white head would emerge from the bottom of the funnel; it somehow appeared to be much smaller than that of the large squawking, flapping bird that had just been pulled out of the chicken crate. The bird's head would pop out of the funnel's neck. Tony would ask, "Do you want the blood?"

More often than not, and especially if the customer was an "old-timer," the answer was yes; and she'd produce a jar with a lid. It made a good blood cake when fried, with a pinch of salt and maybe some oregano flakes and some bread. The end for the chicken was quick and painless. Patsy could do it even in his sleep. The blood flowed from the chicken into the open-glass canning jar, with the name Ball scripted on it; the jar had a matched glass lid.

While the girls would cringe and look away, the boys gawked in awe.

A few minutes to drain and then the bird was placed into one of four boiling kettles on Patsy's little four-jet gas stove by the trough. Not long, a minute or two, it was supposed to loosen the feathers for plucking and the eventual gutting. It certainly did that! Then back to trough for plucking and gutting.

On this particular Saturday the kids witnessed such an execution. It so happened they had walked in at the same time the old lady with the jar (if not a step sooner), but respect for the elders plus Patsy's profits demanded the elder be serviced first. Patsy naturally recognized the kids and knew that their order was ready and cooling on the ice in the back room.

Before wrapping the lady's bloodless chicken, Patsy half rinsed his hands at the nearby water tap and wiped them on his apron. As if it was a sanitary cue, one of the older female cousins scolded the young boy, "Blow your nose, will ya!" Patsy lit up his De Napoli; it was a good day, and he'd probably close before three today.

He lit up, keeping the yellow/orange flame just a tad beneath the end of the cigar and inhaling rapidly. The gray/blue smoke engulfed his face and the golf hat that he wore. ("Blow your nose . . . will ya?") The kid had a cold. ("*Whadda* ya want?") Like his cousins he was mesmerized by the man's head disappearing in the blue-gray smoke of the stogie. Not just him, but his cousins and most of the girls were watching this phenomenal display. The boys were wide-eyed, unblinking, like when that white chicken unselfishly satisfied the old lady's request. The smoke dissipated, somewhat, or a least until the next time Patsy drew on his cigar.

In those days, there were two major tabloids from New York City: The *Mirror* and the *Daily News*. On Sundays both would have color feature sections, normally showing a movie celebrity or sports hero on the front page/cover. At one time the *Daily News* showed a Hollywood siren named Yvonne De Carlo, and there it was, hanging between the sacrificial funnels over the trough and the four kettles of boiling water.

One of the older girls who could read the name in the lower left-hand corner of the picture, (not Antoinette, she wasn't that brave) asked Patsy, "Who is that lady?"

In his best English, which was far from good, Patsy answered, "*Dats* my gugina!"

REALLY!!! . . . nah . . . can't be . . . that's Hollywood . . . a zillion miles away . . . how could his cousin be there making movie pictures? How? It's Patsy the Chicken Man . . . how can that be?

All the kids gawked at the techno color picture of the Hollywood starlet. Then back to Patsy, who by this time had interlaced his fingers under the bib of his apron, showing only the tips of his thumbs and was inhaling deeply on his De Napoli. His face, head and hat, all once again disappeared in blue-gray smoke. The older girls wondered if he was serious; the younger boys only thought, *Wow!* (Blow your nose, will ya?) The homemade handkerchief, made from remnants of the textile mill's waste, was already very damp and sticky. (*Whadda* ya want? I got this code!)

Patsy's apron was a little bloody. He made it a practice to put a clean apron on every Friday morning; but by the time Saturday afternoon rolled around, it was not sparkling white. Patsy gave the kids the four packages of chickens (with the liver, heart, and stomachs), all neatly wrapped and bound. The five girls and the three younger boys, all walked home. It was their neighborhood and they were safe.

They shared the load. (Blow your nose, will ya?) One of Zia Lucia's kids helped Antoinette with Zia Chiara's chicken. They went up to the second-fl oor front. The two girls were rewarded with a glass of watered-down lemonade. "Donnette, you gotta clean the toilet. Thank you, Teresa, remind your mother we are going to the seven-thirty Mass tomorrow at Mt. Carmel, okay?"

"Okay," Teresa replied.

The two bundles that contained some meat for the Sunday sauce and fat and flavor for Monday's soup lay on Zia Grazia's kitchen table. Zia Grazia looked at Young Tony and said, "Antonio, you are a big boy, carry this package up to your mother." "Yeah, sure . . ."

The package tucked securely in his folded arms, Tony made it safely to the third floor (front). His mother said, "Bravo, Antonio . . . what a big boy you are . . . Bravo!" She took the bundle and put it on the kitchen table. She unwrapped it, carefully placing the liver, stomach, and heart on a plate, and grabbed the bird by the neck and one of the legs. She went to the stove and gas jets. Her husband was reading the newspaper; she asked him if he would ignite the gas jet for her. He put his Lucky Strike into a tire like rimmed ashtray (Goodyear), got up, lit a match, and turned the jet on. The jet exploded into an orange and yellow and blue flame. She stepped up to the burning jets, the sacrificial beast in her hands, and started the purification process. Young Tony watched, saw the little chicken hairs crackle and ignite, and wondered what that funny smell was. It was so much later in life that he finally found out.

Wine Making

The grapes would come in flimsy wooden crates in two sizes: thirty-six pounds and forty-two pounds. The crates were stacked and displayed from maybe the first week in September to mid-October; wine lasts forever; juicy grapes become raisins. The types of grapes sold had exotic names like zinfandel, a cuccamagua, niagara and muscatel which could easily be purchased by his father and uncles and goombas all up and down Bleecker Street. The crates would be stacked on the sidewalks in the early hours of the morning and packed away into a truck that evening to be taken away to a "safe" place.

Regardless of the type or size or whom you bought them from, those grapes would attach hordes of pesky little fruit flies, especially when the crates were first stored in the cellar. They would haunt and harass the wine makers during the crushing, squeezing, and working (first aging) process. The swarms would subside gradually, ebbing away ever so slightly on a daily basis and be (almost) completely gone when Tony's father would force the top two-inch circular tong into the barrel's loading hole. With a lit candle, he would make sure its dripping would fall and jell around the outer circumference of the bung and the inner circumference of the barrel's opening. Never leaving his good fortune (2 fifty-five-gallon barrels) to chance or luck, he'd repeat the lighted candle ritual for the next three consecutive nights. The barrels would then be completely airtight.

After the proper aging time, his father would take a barrel spigot, usually made of tubular oak with a twisting handle, place the nose of the spigot on the three-quarter inch "corked" drain opening (near the bottom face of the barrel), and with a flick of his wrist, as sure and as true a sculptor's stroke, drive the nose of the spigot into the full wine barrel. The cork that once held the wine in and the air out was forced into the barrel and would merely float to the top.

The process of wine making, as Tony remembered it, was fairly simple: first of all, he and his brothers had to help carry all those boxes down into the cellar. "Ya gotta stack 'em straight and even, ya hear?"

Then his father would open the first box with the claw of a carpenter's hammer, lift the box, and dump its contents into the crusher. One of his sons would start to crank the large iron wheel—it had a wooden-handle grip. The boys took turns cranking. The best way to describe the crusher would be to say it was square at the top and a slightly smaller square at the bottom, a simple hopper. It did, however, have two vertical iron cylinders: twelve inches in length and a diameter of four inches at the base that was geared to interlace with one another. The space between the two rotating gears was not more than an inch—an inch and a half. (If you see any leaves in the hopper or in the crates, throw them out!)

There was only one crusher in the neighborhood and it belonged to Goomba Colette. If he wasn't using it, one could borrow it. Within a day—day and a half most—the grapes were crushed and starting to "work" in the open-ended (vertical) barrels. Tony had never again inhaled and smelled that aroma, since those days in the cellar. (And yeah! He has been to wineries in California's Napa Valley, along the Hudson River and in Pennsylvania . . . it's not the same!)

When done with the crusher, it would be thoroughly cleaned and the metal parts coated with good olive oil and returned to Goomba's cellar but never, never ever without a small sign of gratitude, maybe two glass quarts of canned tomatoes or maybe a small doily that Tony's mother recently crocheted. A little something to show appreciation.

The grapes all mashed and swimming in the open barrel, Tony's father would order, "*Fa la reposaire* (let it rest)," and in the same breath he'd advise his sons that the wine has got to "work." It seemed an oxymoron, but translated/explained, we could now rest (after the crusher was cleaned and returned) and the natural sugars in the grapes would start to ferment—work, boil.

The open-ended standing barrel was covered with a damp burlap cloth upon which was placed a crude circular wooden cover and a concrete cinder block placed directly in the center. All that and just above it, a swarm of fruit flies. Even if it wanted to, it wouldn't be going anywhere.

Within a few days, it would start to work. The sides of the barrels would be warm to the touch and if one puts his ear up to the barrel wall, he could hear a faint bubbling sound. Sometimes when Tony's brothers came home from school, changed into "outside play clothes," they'd sneak down to the cellar. Carefully they would remove the cinder block, the homemade wooden circular cover, pull off the burlap, and look down into that dark abyss. The aroma was distinct, and the bubbling boiling sound louder; and if one looked closely, he could see broken and squashed pieces of grapes floating on the top of the working liquid. He could see little half balls of liquid slowly appearing and then bursting all over, all over.

Tony's older brother could look right over the rim and into the barrel; his other brother had to stand on tiptoes just to get his nose to the rim and had to stretch his neck to see the show. Tony scrambled around for a sturdy wooden crate. Finding something he quickly moved to the barrel. He climbed upon it, and gripping the rim of the barrel with his fingers, he was now also able to see the spectacle. The wine was boiling and cooking and smelling all at the same time.

"Wow! We're *gunna* make wine!"

The boys eventually broke away from it all, replaced the covering, and went out to play. They'd be back again tomorrow to check it out. As they were leaving Tony looked back and saw that the flies were starting to return to the cinder block, the wooden cover, and the burlap.

When the time was right, and only Tony's father knew, another process took place. It was the transfer of the liquid and mash from the vertical open-ended barrels. The liquid was carefully poured into the horizontal barrel through a bungee hole at the top. His father had a large funnel and he placed a piece of screen inside it at the bottom of the funnel and above its neck. (You don't want any grape skins or seeds in your wine, do you?)

His father would stand on an old Coca-Cola soda case, reach deep down into the open-ended barrel, and would scoop out the purple liquid with a long-handled two-quart cooking pot. Carefully he would hand it to one of his elder sons; the eldest would get a pot that was three-quarts filled; the middle son, a little more than half. (Ya *hadda* work with two pots! It made it go easier and a lot faster!)

In turn, the boys would clutch the pot handle with two hands and in a deathlike grip step over to the vertical barrel and the large funnel, raise the pot shoulder high, and twist their wrist. That was the hardest and most important step for them—the moment of truth, no place for an accident or slip up. His father would later tell their mother the boys "*Hai fatto buono!* (They did well!)".

Tony had the best job during this procedure; he became his father's cowboy. His father would straddle him on the barrel near the center and facing the large funnel. It was the cowboy's duty to watch the purple gold liquid slush, foam, and eventually drop into the abyss beneath the inserted temporary screen and the funnel's neck. He also steadied the funnel during the dangerous pouring step. From his perch on horseback, Tony would occasionally look over the lip of the funnel and squint down into it and check to see if there were any grape skins or seeds accumulating on the screen. If so, the unacceptable material was quickly removed and deposited into a nearby empty coffee can.

When his father finished scooping out as much as he could with the long-handle pot, the last few pot fulls required him to tip the barrel slightly and reach deep; he then would realign the barrel in an upright position. The open-ended barrel rested on two planks. The two planks rested on cinder blocks that gave the barrel about a twelve-inch platform. Just enough for that washtub to fit directly beneath the inch-and-a-half cork on the bottom of the barrel. The same washtub which incidentally was used to soak socks and underwear (in bleach, of course) less than three days ago.

With a piece of an old broomstick, his father would drive this cork into the barrel. Tony held his breath, fearing that a gush would come out, but it didn't. The mash, the previous crushed grapes and stems, had already settled during the initial "aging-work period" and acted as a plug. It did not gush, only a fast spurt at first and then subsiding to a quiet trickle. What escaped into the tub was quickly added to the horizontal barrel. The piece of broomstick handle was substituted for the driven-out inward cork.

"Wow! We are making wine! The best wine this side of Cisternino!"

Funny thing, his father would always call a wine press a "torque"—must be because of the ratchet action at the top. To this day, if Tony sees a wine press, he would refer to it as a torque. Another American word he never freely adapted into his vocabulary was *calendar;* to him it was always *scolla pasta* (pasta drain).

The open-ended barrel would be tipped again, and the overworked long-handled pots were pressed into service once more. His father would start scooping out the mash and putting it into the circular cage of the wine press. The circular cage, with its wooden bars, was like all others Tony had seen then and now. At its diameter opposite points were two iron attachments on a permanent hinge, the other a separate easily removed long iron pin that would drop through "the right, left, right, left" ring openings permanently attached to the cage. When the pin was inserted, the cage was a perfect circle; when removed, the cage walls could swing apart and be taken away. It does make removal much easier. Like the aging timing, it was only his father who said, "*Basta . . . tirare lo spillo* (Enough, pull the pin.)"

Upon filling the cage with liquidly juicy grape skins and pulp, (checking to see if the pin was secure) a thick wooden circular plate was placed onto the cage. It fit solidly and firmly. The plate itself had a large cast-iron flange in the center, with a six-inch diameter screwed into the wood. The torque stem was threaded.

The older boys would start ratcheting the torque, the young first then the older and then the father. Young Tony would plant himself on the floor support beams of the torque to keep it stable. "Wow! We're making wine . . . not just any wine . . . but the best wine this side of Cisternino!"

The mash started to compress; the purple juices oozed out from the cage bars, onto the slightly pitched tray beneath it and rushed to the front, and the future wine would tumble into the washtub. It would flow nice and steady at first, but not later. The liquid content of the washtub was poured into the barrel and returned to its place beneath the torque's spout. (The same one used to soak socks and underwear overnight—just a couple of days ago.)

Tony's father was the last one on the torque. When it became too hard to pull, he'd say, "*Fa la repose* (Let it rest)." A few minutes later, they'd do it again; Angelo first, Salvatore second, and then his father. Tony, the cowboy, resumed his post as the anchor.

The process was repeated, the scooping of the mash into the cage, resetting the pin, alternate pullers, pulling of the pin, and the emptying of the washtub. "*Basta . . . tirare lo spillo!* Wow! We're making wine . . . the best wine this side of Cisternino . . . this side of all of Italy!"

Page Down

A quiet Sunday afternoon, Tony was gently rocking on the glider out in the enclosed porch. His sons were with him, and they were talking about everything and nothing. The boys were smoking their Marlboros and he was smoking his De Napoli. He had come to enjoy a good Tuscany cigar of late but only on Sundays and only with half of a glow on. He had been a heavy Camel (nonfilter) cigarette smoker in the past (so was his brother Sal), and he could easily recite the place, date, and time he quit. He often told his friends, "I was not a nonsmoker but a smoker who didn't smoke." The bluish gray cigar smoke reminded him of so many men in his past. His father and Uncle Mike smoked cigarettes—his father, Lucky Strikes; Zio Mike (the kids would make it half Italian and half English), Camels—way before filter cigarettes, maybe only Kools.

Tony could sing a litany of the Pardi or De Napoli smokers in his long-ago past: Uncle Dan, Uncle Joe, Uncle Serafino, Patsy the Chicken Man, Joe and Dominick Lucarelli, Fridone, Bull Dog, Papa Tony, Old Roxie at the candy store, the tough and mean Tony (with a scar on his cheek) Marraffa . . . and so on. At this stage in his life, Tony liked the smell of the smoke, liked striking wooden matches to start them burning again. He liked the big, very big clouds of smoke the relighting would create. He liked but didn't know why that feeling he got when he kept puffing, puffing away long after it was necessary. (Must be East Utica in your blood, kid!)

His boys were drinking beer, Old Mud and Bud; he had just opened a bottle of Chianti. (The hard stuff was for later after the macaroni (a wedge of locotelli cheese and cheese grater on the table), after the meatballs, sausage, barscolo, the crusty bread and "vinegary" salad, after the Sambuca with three coffee beans floating on the top (past, present, future), after *un poco de dolce* (something sweet), a fruit, a cannoli, a biscotti, long after the very large pasta bowl and the pasta dishes were cleared off the table, then he would say like those real men of his youth, "Gimme 'bout two fingers in a clean glass." His wife or one of his children would promptly comply.

Back on his suburbia screened in porch and to the discussion about everything and nothing, rocking a little bit on the glider, feeling flush in the cheeks and warm inside, Tony would tell his kids about those wooden grape crates. "After making the wine," he'd tell them again (and through an alcoholic haze, did he see their eyes roll? Had he told this story before?), "we weren't done! We'd save everything! Everything!" He would take another sip of the hard stuff, look at their faces, and continue, "Pa would tell us to pull out the nails from the grape crates, then stack the slats and then stack the three-quarter-inch pine ends. Ya *dink* we were done? No way!"

"My father would tell us to straighten out the nails. My brothers and I would sit on the cold concrete basement floor (some tenement houses had dirt floors). We'd pinch, twist, and align those little pesky inch-and-a-half nails with one hand. The other hand held a hammer, and we'd bang out the 'bumps and curves in the nail' (Watch your fingers, will ya?). The realigned nails were then dumped into an empty coffee can, the same one used earlier when keeping the funnel screen clear. Sitting on the cold concrete cellar floor probably did not help our future hemorrhoids; but Pa ended up with three quarters of coffee can filled with mostly straightened wooden nails, which was good; who knows when you'll need some?" (*Dat's* important!)

Tony would puff on his cigar and rock slowly on the glider and take another sip of the hard stuff. He'd watch the smoke curl around his face and slowly drift upward. He'd tell his kids, "They were the good days in East Utica."

A respectful pause, another sip of the hard stuff, his sons, also out of respect, only tasted the froth of their beers and waited. Tony repeated, "Yeah, they were the good old days!"

Finally one of his sons said, "Dad, look around you; these are good days too!"

The other quickly chimed in, "Yeah, look around ya? You got more property than half of the 900 block of Catherine Street . . ."

The other son came back in, saying, "You got an arbor like Goomba Colette, a garlic and a tomato patch like Don Alberto's; a pear tree like the Lebanese Mike Nassar, so many pears you throw half of them back into the garden to rot and feed the soil; you got four rose plants for Mom, *whaddya* want?"

He didn't know. He didn't reply.

They, both sons, reminded him that he never did leave East Utica; he only dragged it with him, like the immigrants and their patron saints.

Still he didn't know and took another sip. (His wife was right; he drinks too much.)

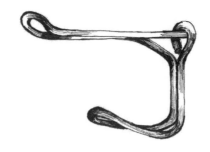

Clothes Line . . . Brownstone . . .

Page Up Page Down

It was a three-story brownstone (they used to call it brick) with only six apartments, two on each floor in tandem. It was small by normal standards because the original builders were limited by the lot size. The backyard had one pole, about the size and height of a telephone pole with climber spikes about every two feet. The pole stood at the very end of the property. There were three crossbars (two-by-fours) nailed horizontally about five feet in length and roughly corresponding in height to the three stories of the brownstone. On the end of each crossbar were two metal pulleys with clothesline (rope) running back to three rear hallway windows of the brownstone. Each apartment had one clothesline for their own use (unless the *patrone* (landlord) had an extra large load of laundry), and it was the tenants' responsibility to maintain their designated line and pulleys. The little boy remembers his father climbing the pole to the highest crossbar and slipping the line through the pulley. Coming back to the building, he'd tie the ends of the clothesline to a very long string that his mother held on to up at the third-story window. His mother would then carefully pull the line up, and when she got up to their hallway window, he and his father were already up the two flights of stairs. Tony's father would run the line into the pulley that was attached to the building and tightly knot the ends, making sure there was no slack in the line. The line would in time sag by the weight of the weekly (sometimes biweekly) washes. You could always smell the bleach on laundry days.

In the years that followed, Tony would still feel frightened at the memory of his father climbing and climbing and climbing that pole with a rope tied to his belt loop—up to the third crossbar, close to the sky where God and all the saints lived. The higher he got, the more the pole would sway; and it terrified the boy deeply. The boy wanted to call out, "Pa, . . . Pa, . . . come down . . . please come down . . . please!" But he couldn't, all he could do was watch with his stomach and chest constrained into big knots, causing him to pant in short, quick breaths.

The brownstone had three front porches facing the street. Families renting the rear apartments had two balconies for the second and third floor. A large concrete stoop with three steps on each end acted as porch for the first-floor tenants and the "rear" entrance for the second and third-floor tenants. The stoop and balconies were not in the rear of the brownstone, but three-quarters of the way down the alley on the west side of the structure. The balconies were like shelves sticking out of the building. They had no vertical post supporting them, only four triangular-angle iron braces that supported the floor of the balconies. The floors acted as roofs for the bottom stoop and the second-floor balcony. The third floor got the alfresco accommodations. The back stoop once had been graced with two-inch iron-pipe railings, but the boy never saw them, only some rusty pipe in the empty post holes there on the concrete stoop. They seemed to act as silent ruins of a once-grander time—like the Acropolis or Roman and Greek amphitheaters. The front porches were all made of wood except for the base/stoop of the ground-floor porch. That was made of solid cement and had six steps; no handrail. The front porches, all supported by rounded posts, had roofs, even the third floor. The tenants would often bring out stools and homemade benches to catch any air movement outside, especially on those hot July and August nights. The front door to the brownstone was a heavy wooden door painted gray since Columbus discovered America, with a three-foot square glass plate in the upper portion.

Once inside the front door, and to the immediate left (five feet above the floor and nailed on to the hallway wall) was a communal mailbox (black) only wide enough to hold letters. Anything larger the mailman would leave on the floor directly below. As far back as any one of the guys could remember, the mailbox had its top hinge/lid missing. However, there was evidence (like the rear stoop's empty posts holes) that the mailbox was once grand and complete. The lidless half mailbox served its main purpose: a holding area for all the tenants. The amputation of the total grandeur did, however, have a big plus. A person only had to look and could easily see if there was anything in the mailbox—or under it.

That solitary, regular size, indoor, mutilated mailbox, which in its lifetime held draft notices from the Selective Service, letters form the Old Country announcing births and deaths and other news, letters from Korea, Germany, the Pacific, the gas and electric bill (Niagara-Mohawk did both), etc., was relatively exposed.

When you think about it, it was strange. The tenants never left their stools or chairs or homemade benches on any of the porches, balconies, or stoops overnight. Never.

The mail remained in a communal box, right out there on the other side of the outside door, easily accessible to man or beast. It must have been a matter of priorities.

Page Down

Tony's daughter was asked to be a bridesmaid and her husband an usher. The wedding was going to take place in Toronto, Canada. Tony and his wife were invited to the ceremony and decided to make it an extended weekend. His wife even booked one night at the Sky-dome Stadium Hotel. The picture windows of the room overlooked the right field. What a rush, even if it was for only one night of a four-day stay. The Yankees were not in town (it was the Florida Marlins) but still, imagine sitting in a plush (by Tony's standards) motel room with a complete service bar and watching a Sunday afternoon ball game? Tony recalled the lyrics to an old song, "If they could only see me now!" His daughter and son-in-law joined them to see the game, and they (mostly Tony) almost emptied the service bar. Good time, no complaints, he'd do it again in a heartbeat; that's how Tony thought of the experience.

On that particular trip/sojourn to Toronto, they (Tony and his wife and the kids, when available) did some sightseeing and touring: big Greek population in this town, a great subway system, big Chinese settlement, and a good-size "Little Italy." Tony and the "mama" went to Little Italy one afternoon and had a great time, doing the little shops, looking for grappa. They bought a pendulum picture frame that had three individual (circular) frames attached and hung straight down. When they finally got home Tony's wife immediately dug out pictures of her parents' wedding, her and Tony's wedding picture (a snapshot) and a picture of Tony's parents with their firstborn baby, Tony's older brother. Tony's parents were married in Italy, and he never saw photos (if any ever existed) of their wedding.

The latter photo was from a professional studio. *You gotta remember,* Tony thought, *way back in those days when my older brother was a toddler, the old Kodak Box camera wasn't readily available to mill workers and they would have to go to a "professional photographer" on Bleecker Street, like Baleno's Studio or Modern Studio.* His parents dressed their child in his finest and they themselves in their Sunday's best and would walk (they'd only use the trolley for going way downtown) to one of those studios. They'd pose for maybe a set of six pictures. About a week later, a selection was made from the earlier posed pictures, which came in an eight-by-five-inch yellowish manila envelope with the photographer's name, his Bleecker Street address, and Utica 3, NY proudly printed in the upper left corner of the envelope. Not all the businesses on Bleecker Street had phones, and those that did, their phone number contained a mere five digits. Those photos were called "proofs" and looked very purplish, and were extremely sensitive to light. A decision being made, his parents would order one for each of the families in America, several copies for the "old country" and one for the house. The "house" picture and the many family group pictures that followed were carefully stowed away by Tony's mother in a store-bought photo album. The front and rear covers were made of a thick sort of granulated dark green cardboard, the pages were black construction-type paper, and all had two holes punched on the extreme left side. A black shoelace would run through the covers and pages and be neatly bowed on the front. On the cover and in the center, in silvery colored ink written in script was "Album".

Tony ended up with the album after his mother passed on. He is hesitant, maybe melancholic about it and seldom goes to it. He does, however, often stop and study the faces in the circular pendulum picture frames that they picked up in Toronto. His daughter resembles his mother, especially about the forehead, her eyes, her lips, her chin and her curly/wavy hair. Tony thinks his daughter is one of the most beautiful girls alive. And who do you think that would surprise?

That evening (the day Tony and his wife purchased the pendulum frame) his wife and daughter really wanted to have dinner on top of the Canadian National Railroad Tower. It looked a zillion feet high. Tony begged off but readily gave his blessing to his wife and daughter and son-in-law. His son-in-law inquired why, and Tony just said, "Aw . . . it's probably too expensive for my blood, and I prefer to have a couple of hot dogs from the venders . . . and do some people watching . . . Don't worry I'll be by the elevators when you come down." Tony thought, *I'll bet by the time they get on the elevator, my wife and daughter would have filled him in as to why I wouldn't go.*

He watched them all get on the elevator and go up to the sky, to where God lives and all the saints. He closed his eyes and turned away, because if he watched too much longer, he knew he would see the superstructure sway. Even seeing the elevator go up a lousy fifty feet terrified and frightened him. The tightness in his stomach, the weakening of his knees, a feeling of dizziness, and the sensation of falling made Tony angry and ashamed of himself. The anger was easy to handle, it's the shame that's not.

Even before his daughter was born, Tony and his two boys went to Niagara Falls; and part of the sightseeing included a trip up the Seagram Tower; at that time he was unaware of his phobia. He remembered it being a very hot and muggy August evening, and strangely he got a little wheezy going up that elevator. When they got to the top, there was a steady and gusty wind blowing; the wind was refreshing, but the wheezing continued. Tony stayed close to the elevator doors, pressing the back of his shoulders to the elevator walls. The boys and his wife ventured out on the platform, the wind blowing her hair and the boys dashing to the railing to see the panorama of the city lights below them, way below them. Tony got frightened;, the kids and his wife were disappointed when after what seemed like weeks to him, and probably only five minutes to them, Tony said, "Let's go . . . the ice cream is on me."

Then again a couple of years later, only this time the Empire State Building. "When the hell are you going to learn, Tony?" The same wrenching feeling in his stomach, his knees were going wobbly and now he was experiencing dizziness. Changing elevators, trying not to think of those miles and miles of iron-twisted cables, the rapidly spinning pulleys, going up unbelievably swiftly, he thought, *Let the pulleys hold God . . . please don't let the line snap off and break . . .* And he remembered, *Please, Pa, come down . . . please come down . . . please . . .*

Page Up

The heavy wooden door with the three-by-three glass plate in the upper portion had numbers nailed to it directly underneath it: a metal number nine, a blank, and then another metal number two. If one looked closely and studied it, he could make out the outline of a number under the layers of gray enamel paint—number one. This was 912 Catherine Street.

Once you passed the lidless mailbox on your left, you face a hallway, about seven to eight feet wide. The left half was a staircase, sixteen wooden steps, with a handrail and the bottom post; the handrail had an acorn proudly placed upon it, for beauty and elegance. In the halls, the walls to the left and the walls to the right, had forty-eight inches of wainscoting and plaster finish to the ceiling. Everything was painted gray, the wainscoting a darker shade. The staircase had a banister with sixteen spindles, painted (surprise!) gray. The rear staircase had the seventh spindle missing since before Tony or anyone else could remember, high enough for a skinny kid to squeeze through and jump/drop five to six feet down on to the hallway floor. Tony had trouble doing that.

All the walls and all the woodwork were painted with oil-based enamel paint. (So much for lead poisoning in those days.)

At the top of the front-door flight of stairs (both second and third story) was a large double-hung window to the right (opening out to the alleyway), and to the left was the kitchen door of a tenant's apartment. To the rear, it was just the reverse; only the hallway window was the door to the balconies. The rear double-hung windows opened on to the backyard and was where the tenants put their pulleys and clotheslines—one on each side of the window.

Each flat had five rooms and a bath. The long and somewhat narrow kitchen had two double-hung windows on the far side and the bathroom on the near side. The cast-iron white porcelain-covered bathtub had four eagle-talon-type clawed support legs no more than six inches in height. Tony's mother was always proud of the fact that the flat did not only have its very own toilet, but a bathtub too for their exclusive use! (Some tenant houses required two families to use one common toilet, and no bathtub whatsoever.)

His mother lived in that tenement house for fifty-seven years. Every room, including the bathroom, was linoleum over wood. There was a hand braided floor mat at the kitchen sink (*la pompa*) and another in the bathroom between the bathtub, toilet, and wash basin sink. The linoleum was always cool to the touch and always very cold in the dead of winter.

There were four rooms off the kitchen, two on each side. It was a cold-water fl at (no central heating/furnace) but it did have a manually operated gas-fired hot-water tank. His mother was proud of that too! What a blessing on bath nights or laundry days; once again, not all brownstones had that luxury. A very large black cast-iron stove with four gas jets on the right side and a deep coal fire box with a grate/shaker at the bottom were on the left. This was the only source of heat in the winter as well as cooking and baking year-round. Yes and one more thing, it would become the clothes dryer all winter and on inclement days in the fall and spring.

Tony's father once bought his mother a wooden indoor clothes dryer. It was designed to be hung vertically when not in use, and his father attached it high up on the door frame by and over the stove. There was a hinge near the top and it had eight rods attached to it. The rods were only permanently attached at the hinge, but the bottom of the rods was unattached, thus being able to swing freely when propped up. When not in use it appeared (if you have a child's imagination) to be a huge woodpecker, holding himself on to a tree trunk, listening (twisting its head back forth) for bugs in the bark of a tree. Its wings tucked tightly about his back and sides, bobbing its head back and forth way over the very warm, sometimes hot fire box of the big black stove.

When in use, however, the rods were propped up and spread wide, making a half circle over the big black coal stove like a hawk soaring over a kill.

Tony's mother, because of her petite frame, had to stand on a chair in order to hang those socks, underwear, work trousers, an occasional dress and apron, and so on. The laundry basket, which contained the just-washed batch of clothing (is that bleach I still smell?), was placed on the nearby kitchen table. Antoinette or Little Tony or one of his brothers would help.

Helping little hands would go to the laundry basket, pick out an item, snap some of the moisture out of it, and hand it to his mother. "No, not that one, Tony . . . I don't have enough room on this stick. Give me a sock. *Se! Quello!* (Yes, that one!) Good boy, Tony!"

Tony remembered sensing and feeling the heat generated by the deep coal box and his mother's hand reaching as if to steer young Tony further away from the hot coal fire and that sad smile, under even sadder eyes that told him, "Careful, watch out for the hot stove! Bravo Antonio! Now step away from the stove. Good boy!" He would quickly return to the laundry basket and retrieve yet another damp piece of clothing. He would snap the moisture out of it and with two hands hold it up like offering a sacrifice and await his mother's approval or consent.

Page Down

Tony had just opened a bottle of Chianti and stepped out on his back porch. (*Ah, suburbia life!*) Both wine bottle and glass in hand (glass held upside down), he settled into hi favorite "outside lawn chair." He then looked around for one of his Tuscany Sunday cigars. He poured a finger or a finger and a half of wine into the glass, sniffed it, and tasted it, keeping his lips tightly closed and swishing the wine under his tongue and around his gums. He popped his lips, forcing air into his mouth and tried to feel or sense the sensation of the liquid on his tongue and taste buds. *Not bad,* he thought, *and like they used to say in the old neighborhood, "There is wine and there is vinegar . . . and no such thing as bad wine!"* He half smiled at the simplicity of the old saying.

Not thinking of anything special, he looked around a bit and wondered, Whats dat? . . . Dare *on the maple? Ah, it's* nuttin', *just a stupid squirrel . . .* nah, it ain't . . . It's a woodpecker . . . One of **dose** black and gray and white kind . . . They got a name . . . My wife's cousin told me, but I don't remember . . . look at that thing? Climbing up and down, sideways and backward . . . head first downward . . . then quickly up right . . . pretty to watch . . . It can move *laterally as well as it can move up and down. Sometimes you've got to click your heels together and move sideways . . . to get ahead and move forward.*

In the blink of an eye, the animal was airborne and gone. Tony sipped a little bit of his wine and remembered that just before the woodpecker vanished, it assumed the upright position, wings tucked in around its back and flanks. He blurted out, "What the hell does that remind of? I know! The burst of the wingspan of Joey's pigeon or the wooden clothes dryer being open on wash days. Yeah . . . *dat's* it!"

He took another sip of the grape and wondered, *the woodpecker is now free! It can go wherever it wants . . . do what ever it wants! Free!* **Free?** *But is it really free? Is there an instinct in that creature that has no soul? Is there something akin to responsibility? The nest. the young, the family? Nothing? Free? Free from what?*

Tony wasn't sure of the answer. He took another sip of the grape.

The Scissors . . . Fresh Fish

Page Down

Tony was sitting at the glass-top picnic table, which he hated but his wife loved. (Too many things wrong with the goddamn table; it's too big; those damn half-canvas, half-wrought iron chairs don't fit good under the table. It would be all right if you put it in the middle of Yankee Stadium—but not here!)

He despised it and despised it with an unholy passion out there on the back porch. "That lousy patio set . . . (with its six clumsy chairs, two of which are on large circular bases and weighing a couple of tons) is just too big and awkward for this porch. The porch isn't that small, but it is narrow like Ma's kitchen on Catherine Street . . . *Bella, ma un poco stretto* (Nice but a little narrow)."

He came out to clip his fingernails—damn!—and said, "Why do I have so much trouble doing this with my left hand than I do when the clipper is in my right hand? I guess we really are creatures of habit . . . or is it dexterity? Or is it? You know! Quit bullshitting yourself . . . joint ache and rheumatism. Whatever, it's a bitch doing!"

Then he admitted it to himself, "*Naw! You always had trouble clipping left-handed . . . who you kidding? . . . And toenails are even worse . . . even right-handed.*"

Clipping his fingernails always put Tony in a negative mood. (Don't ask why . . . it just did!)

Suddenly he smirked, then loosened up, and then smiled broadly, "Ma's scissors! Just one pair . . . all those years . . . one pair . . . multi-duties!" He started to feel less ornery.

Page Up

Friday was bath night; Monday, laundry day; Sunday, Tuesday, and Thursday were macaroni days with meat sauce (the meat plate got less abundant as the week progressed), a routine developed, a comfort zone with an outside perimeter; one knew when and what to expect.

And because it was yesterday, life was good.

La fru-ja (the scissor) was a beautiful thing. Friday morning Tony's mother went out with Zia Grazia to Tony Marraffa's fish market; they got five pounds of *murlutz* (whitees) from the man who had a long scar on his right cheek. "I'll clean all of them for only fifteen cents . . . I clean them good!" the short scar-faced man said.

"*Non! Noi siamo da Vasto!* (No, we are from Vasto—on the Adriatic) We know and understand fresh fish!"

Tony's uncles often told him that Vasto (once called Hostium) predated Rome. No! Those stout, strong women could easily clean their own fish, and in all probability as good, if not better than he ever could. (Besides, maybe they'd use the fish heads as a broth/base for some soup. Uncle Dan loved and enjoyed any sort of sea food meal.)

At that time Zia Grazia's family lived at the second floor front flat. The women from Vasto returned home and upon turning into the alleyway, they spotted the kids playing within its narrow confines. "Donnetta, here is the key. Go home and get me the blue bowl and the scissors. Bring them to Zia Chiara's house . . . and don't forget to lock the door on the way out." And as an after thought Donnetta's mother added, "And don't slam the screen door!"

"Okay, Ma," she replied. Gathering her skip rope, she ran ahead of her mother and her aunt, folding the rope as she moved down the alleyway and up the rear stairs. She stuffed her skip rope into her pocket, completed the mission, and was waiting with bowl and scissor in hand when the women from Vasto arrived at Tony's door.

Back to the brownstone, up the rear staircase, the package of fresh fish finally came to rest in the center of Tony's mother's kitchen table. The sisters would not only equally divide and share the fish, but also the chore of cleaning and washing them.

His mother cut the string that Tony "Papa de Porco" Marraffa (his nickname in the neighborhood was Pope of the Pigs) had used to wrap the fish. She spread open the wrapping and she tried to keep the contents in the center of the paper. She tried to pile them as neatly as she could, but because fresh fish are always so slippery it was difficult. Tony's mother got out her scissors and a bowl and sat opposite of her sister. And like they once did in Italy as little girls, they started to clean the fish.

Off went the head with a woman's good, solid, firm snap of the scissor blades, putting the head on a designated area of the used wrapping paper; then opening the scissor blades again and with one side she'd run it down the underbelly of the fish, laying it open; then she'd clamp the blades together once more and scrape out the entrails of the fish, depositing the entrails in the center of the wrapping; then she'd flop the fish over on its recently emboweled underside, and with blades opened again, she'd start scraping the scales from the fish.

"Do you want any fish heads?"

"No, I don't think so . . . the boys don't really like it that much; you take them. Donato likes fish soup."

"Okay, but you got to take a couple of these pieces of murlutz from my bowl."

"*Non e necessario*! (It is not necessary!)"

"I insist!"

The waste was quickly and tightly wrapped and disposed of. "Tony take this downstairs and put it into the garbage can in the shed; make sure the lid is on good and put it in deep; when the cats smell what is in there, they'll try hard to get it."

"Okay, Ma." Then Tony asked, "How are you gonna make 'em, Ma, fried or in a sauce?"

She said, "Fried." Tony smiled, (that is the way he preferred them) picked up the smelly bundle, making sure to keep away from his body as much as he could and went out to the garbage shed.

That night, after he and his brother had taken their bath and were sitting in the kitchen barefooted near the warm stove, drying off, the scissor came out again. The three boys—each in turn, each with their individual toes—got a toenail manicure. Their mother had it down to a science: grasp the heel firmly, point the toes upward and toward the ceiling, and snip, snip; and like the fish heads earlier that afternoon, their toenails also became detached from their bodies.

Tony's mother would use that simple, unsophisticated, plain instrument to cut patches from old soon-to-be discarded overalls and mend the knees of those that had a little more life left in them. She once carefully snipped and saved enough white silk from an old blouse and miraculously transformed it into two white purses with draw stings. The purses were given to two of her nieces: Donnetta and Frances. The girls proudly carried their beautiful little gifts, white as new snow, in the crux of their elbows when they walked side by side down the center aisle at St. Anthony of Padua Church with the First Holy Communion class. Hands pressed tightly together, fingers extended fully, encasing their new prayer book; white net veils, the purse gently bobbing as they solemnly walked down to the communion rail. The girls knelt, received their First Communion and were in a *State of Grace*.

It was Ma's scissor that helped Tony (concentrating so much that the tip of his tongue slipped out of the side of his mouth) round the corners on the Christmas card he made for Don Alberto.

"Ya wanna *know* **sumptin**'? *Huh ? Huh ? I tell ya! It's not what ya want dat's gonna make you happy . . . Nah! Not in a zillion years . . . it's what ya do wid what ya got! Dat's what's gonna make ya happy!*"

Porch versus Stoop

Page Down

So?? . . . So what the hell is a porch? Is this a 'porch' in suburbia Allentown/Philadelphia.? But it's got a table . . . porches . . . like stoops . . . don't have tables . . . maybe a chair or a small bench . . . but no tables . . . and not in a zillion years like this one's got either !!! The wife and the kids would be quickly tell you that this is a screened in porch . . . *screened in* . . . (screened in? What the hell? Doesn't that make it a room?) . . . but I guess not here in suburbia Philadelphia/Allentown.

Is this part of *The American Dream? Whaddya want? Whaddya lookin for?*

Ahh !!! . . . But . . . you gotta remember . . . it is a long way from the 900 block of Catherine and the narrow eight foot wide alley way; between the brownstone and Goomba Colette's frame home . . . and the feasts . . . and the lunch pails . . . and the bean picking . . . and the spittoons . . . and the gnumariedi . . . and the chicken store . . . and *"il café nero con un piccolo di coraggio"* (an espresso with some courage) . . . and the snap snap snap of the jump rope striking the concrete walk

Yeah . . . but . . .

Shouldn't a porch, if it's on the ground floor be elevated ??? like a stoop . . . different levels . . . (not a measly four inches . . .) but two, three . . . four, steps enough for kids to sit on and explain to one another the meaning of life. The innocence . . . the confidence of inexperience . . . the sense that every thing is still in front of you . . . little . . . very little . . . if any . . . is behind you. You had it all . . .

in your hands and in your head . . . all of it !! in front of you . . . but now it is gone!!

But you ain't gonna tell me this is a god damn porch!! It's 'snot!!!!

'Snot in a zillion years!!!!

Page Up

The distinct and un-forgettable odors of bleach and moth balls . . . . Ma darning socks . . . by the window in the summer and by the big black warm stove in the winter . . . the wooden clothes tree that collapsed like a woodpecker to the door frame and spread open like a soaring hawk when needed to dry socks and underwear and tee shirts and . . .

Blue jeans . . . over-alls . . . what ever . . . with neat rectangular hand-sown patches on the knees . . . or . . . (the shame of it all!!!) . . . on your butt . . . the steam whistles form the textile mills . . . telling you when to get up and when to go for lunch and when Pa was coming home . . . and . . . only on Sundays . . . *when God won* . . . and you could hear the church bells at the Agnus Dei . . . and you knew Ma was putting the water on for the Sunday macaroni with real meat . . . like braciola and meatballs and sausage and . . . cross your fingers . . . pig tails . . . codini . . . (pig tails . . . all the way to the very end)) and good cheese for the macaroni and bread to wipe up the sauce that was left on the plate . . . and to share the 'one' mop-pean . . . used by all at the table . . .

The kitchen table, like an altar, with wine for Pa, wine and 7up for the kids . . . the family all at the blessed table. Designated kitchen chairs, designated spots, either a fork or a spoon, a plate (more of an oversize soup bowl), a glass, and Ma ladling out the macaroni . . . Pa first Ma last, because the one that serves is the greatest among us. Sunday dinner and the family. *"Make the sign of the cross before you start to eat, you ain't no animal!!! . . . Boy oh boy am I hungry!! This is good!!"*

Page Down

So this is an enclosed porch?

And there is that a bird bath . . . right on the other side of the screen . . . not ten feet away . . . the bird bath that the grand kids help paint and made such a mess that their grandma is still bitchin' about it . . . and there are a couple of woodpeckers that come to the near by huge maple tree and fl utter around . . . and cardinals and wrens and blue jays that come and drink from it . . . and splash around in the bird bath water.

And the blue jays . . . as pretty as they are . . . could be nasty like Mrs. Bailey and Bull Dog . . .

And someone sits there, in the screened in porch watching all this . . . smoking a Tuscany cigar . . . the space around his head fills up with bluish gray smoke . . . it dissipates soon . . . and someone sips a little wine . . . and someone studies the purple rings made on the table top . . . and looks up to see if any birds are at the bird bath . . . and some one rocks slightly wondering which specie will come to drink next.

In Utica . . . the little sparrows . . . brownies we use to call 'em . . . English sparrows . . . they hung around . . . even in the winter . . . these guys didn't jump ship in cold weather . . . they were survivors . . . they could live on junk . . . they'd fl utter around *a wrapped up winterized fig tree and await the promise of spring.'*

Someone draws again on his Tuscany cigar, the red tip glows a bit more brightly, a thick cloud of blue gray smokes circles his head. The cloud quickly spreads and dissipates. It is gone.

Someday, like the smoke, someone will be gone.

Cigars and Fingers

Page Down

Tony went to Goomba Joe's Restaurant. He hoped to
see the Lucerelli cousins, Big John and Little John, same
grandfather same name. Big John worked the kitchen, as
did his father Joe; and Little John worked the bar, as did
his father Dominic. Years at the restaurant qualified both
to interchange roles with ease. It was not only Eli Whitney
or Henry Ford who practiced, studied and developed
interchangeable parts and assembly line technique; i.e.
weapons in the Revolutionary War . . . carcass of cattle in
Chicago stockyards and slaughter houses. No. "Mother"
still remains the need of necessity, and a busy bar/kitchen
has a lot of necessities. Little John was busy at the far end
of the bar, telling a bunch of younger guys of his days in
the army: he was cook, and he was telling about this dumb
rebel who screwed up a rice meal. Big John was stocking
his kitchen with tubs of fried green peppers and tubs of
tomato sauce from the freezer. He wore old army gloves
when he went into the freezer and was heavy clad like he
was a member of Admiral Perry's expedition to the North
Pole. He eventually emerged from the Jay Street tundra,
pulled off his gloves and watch cap, and took off his jacket.
He looked around for a second and then spotted Tony.

"Hey, *whaddaya* doin' up here? Hope it is a wedding
and not a funeral!"

"Naw," Tony answered, "just came up for the PFC club
dinner last night. How you doin', John? Is your daughter
still living on Long Island?" John had only one daughter;

as a matter of fact, both Big John and Little John had only one daughter each.

"Aye!" he answered, raising his right hand behind his right ear. "They moved to Saratoga Springs about five years ago . . ."

"That's good," Tony quickly replied. "The kids are closer, and it gives ya a chance to play the horses once in a while."

"Aye!" he said again. "*Uf-fa* . . . with the ponies . . . no more ponies . . . Me and my wife go out to see the grandkids." No such oral reply was necessary. Tony smiled broadly and just nodded; he knew about grandkids too!

"Hey, John, how did you guys make the gnumariedi in the old days? I had them in Cisternino last time I was there, about two years ago; and they were great, just like the old days here for the feast of Saints Cosmas and Damian."

"Aye!" Big John again with that aye, and added, "We used to get the pig intestines from a couple of slaughter houses, but they dried up and then we got them from a place in West Winfield. But that dried up too! We used calf and pig livers and some parts of the lung; you ain't *gunna* see that any more. They gotta sell it to dog food manufacturers and not to the public; you can't buy it anymore even if you wanted too . . ." He returned to the original question and said, "Then we'd wrapped *dem* in a bay leaf, some parsley, and put them on the spit and roast them. You remember 'subway,' don't ya?"

"Ya betcha *yur* ass I remember! I'll betcha a ten spot it's probably the same clowns that tell ya you can't smoke here or there; you gotta wear your seatbelts; and Christmas mangers in City Hall is politically incorrect, and all that shit! They'd rather feed it the dogs," Tony said and then added with a sneer, "Assholes! They're all fuckin' test-tube babies, if you *axe* me!"

Little John came down to the far end of the bar and said, "Yo, Tony, how you doin'?"

"I'm doin' good, John. How you doin'? And how is that beautiful Victoria?"

Little John named his daughter after his grandmother. Tony remembered her well as another one of those stout women who were always active in church affairs. Little John asked Tony what he wanted. Before Tony answered, a mental picture crossed his mind of Commarra Victoria, and in the same split second Tony remembered that Little John's own mother was not named Victoria. Her name was very Italian sounding (unique to a certain southern Italian area) and the name never was totally absorbed in the next generation of East Uticans. But Victoria was nice and it also showed, to a certain extent, the proper respect that had to be rendered to the family.

Tony also knew that Little John lost his mate early in life, and his mom raised little Vicky. He was sure that Little John had his mother's blessing in naming the pretty girl the way they did. Even the "old-timers" would not have objected—well, not too long anyway.

"Gimme a Wild Turkey and a splash of Pierri with a twist of lime. You wanna drink?" he asked Big John. Just a quick shake of the head was his negative response.

Little John said after hearing Tony's order, "Where the fuck do ya think you're at? This is Joe's, not Philadelphia!"

Tony laughed and said, "All right smart ass, gimme a shot of bourbon and the beer chaser." Tony thought to himself, *So this is what suburbia has done to you, huh? Betcha if ya ordered a shot of bourbon in Philly. I'd probably have to play twenty questions with the bar tender (in all likelihood it would be a bar maid) and another thing, a "shot" at Joe's was a jigger; no bells and whistles; no fruit cocktails; no tiny umbrellas; no fancy stemmed glasses; a shot and a beer like the old days. Just like Bull Dog.*

Tony told Little John, "Put one in the barrel for yourself . . ."

"Naw," he said, "Thanks anyway." And Little John moved down to the other end where the "kids" were still talking and horsing around. As Little John walked away, Tony looked around at all the patrons and thought to himself, *You know, other than Big John here and Little John, of course, there is no one in this room that knows how Little John's daughter got her name, unless maybe he might have told some of 'em. The older you get, the more ghost you have in your thoughts.* Talking about the gnumariedi reminded Tony of Fridone and the giant Finnocchio. He turned to Big John again and asked, "You 'member Fridone and Finnocchio, don't ya? Sure ya do! What ever happened to them guys?"

Big John again answered with his "Aye!" Only this time his right hand went way over his head as if to emphasize his point and show what time can actually do to old sweet memories. He quickly looked up at the tin ceiling and then back to Tony. Then he reported.

"Finnocchio . . . I don't know. I heard a long time ago he moved to Endicott or Fulton or someplace to be closer to a cousin he had *dare* or *sumptin'* . . . Fridone died a sad death . . ."

"What happen to him?" Tony asked. The story unfolded.

"More than twenty five years ago, he was living at the old Venus Bar and Restaurant. He had a room above the bar. One very cold January night, the little man had much too much to drink (obviously not at the Venus) and was walking home—maybe *staggering* would be more descriptive—he must have stumbled more than once or twice. He finally fell into a snow bank and fell asleep.

"They found him the next day, and his left hand was so badly frostbitten they had to amputate four fingers and up to the first joint on his thumb." John continued, "He became a ward of the state and died shortly thereafter."

"Aw, shit!" Tony said. Tony remembered how not only Fridone but all the old-timers would light up their stogies a hundred times and sometimes and in all probability, right here where he was now standing at Joe's bar. They would hold the lit wooden match an inch below the cigar, draw on the cigar, and they could see an orange flame being sucked up to it. With the other hand, they would twist the cigar to get a thorough-glowing hot ember, all 360 degrees. (*Whadda* bummer!) They would snap their wrist to extinguish the flame, and their heads would disappear in a cloud of blue gray smoke.

Tony always liked Fridone and he knew he just knew it, that Fridone liked him. (How did the poor bastard even light up his cigars after losing his fingers? Aw, shit! *Whadda* bummer!)

Tony carefully lifted the shot glass and skimmed the top of it, sipping it slowly. He looked across the room at some of the tables by the windows. (And right there by the second table in from the window is where Finnocchio almost killed Bull Dog.)

Not even the king of England eats as good as this . . . He ain't go no gnumariedis echoed somewhere in the back of Tony's mind.

The floor was now red tile, maybe eight-by-eight or ten-by-ten (if that) squares. Big Johnny got rid of the spittoons the day of his Uncle Dominic's funeral. *So,* Tony thought, *the wooden floor upon which old Fridone dropped his cigar when the Forestieri grabbed his arm, the floor that Bull Dog bounced off with Finnocchio's massive hands around his neck, the floor where Fridone's cigar fell upon . . . and rolled a little and finally came to rest by the white spittoon—it is all here, but it's not!*

In the years to come, Tony would often think of Fridone and Finnocchio, especially when he would light up a Tuscany cigar and roll it with his thumb and fingers under an orange flame, squinting through the blue gray smoke. "*Dose* poor bastards weren't dealt a good hand to play with!"

The Requiem

Carlo's Identification
A Thousand Words . . . Ash Wednesday
Intro to Paulie
Carmen's and Espresso

Carlo's Identification

Page Down

Still another Proctor's Fifties Club monthly dinner meeting at the Sons of Italy . . . fair crowd . . . maybe fifty or sixty. A copy of that old photo was floating around. Carlo Sinisgalli came over to Tony's table and handed him a paper place mat and proudly announced, "I named *'em* all!!!"

Tony voice boomed out saying (much louder than was necessary), "ATTA BOY Carlucci!!! *Atta boy!!! Ya sure? All of 'em??*" (With a little bit of the grape, Tony's raspy voice always increased an octave or two.)

"Yeah I'm sure!!!

"All of *'em? . . . ya sure???*" repeated Tony.

"*Whadda ya* want from me??? I wrote the names on the back of the place mat . . . take a look for yourself you big horse's ass . . . I'm not *gunna* guarantee the spelling but *dose* are the names!!" The guys at the table as well as Tony roared with laughter at Carlo's description of his old friend.

On one side of the placemat were some drawings/photos, Tony flipped it over, and there it was: a roster of names, two groups one entitled, "Back Row' and underlined; the other 'Bottom Row', also underlined. It read:

Back Row

Guy Cristallo
Anthony Dachario
John Rugiero
George Frattasio
Tommy Lisandrelli
Ray Joseph
Fred Tomaino
Jack Del Monte
James Moore
Tony

Bottom Row

Sal Convertino
Pat Caputo
Joe Graziano
Vinny Scalzo
Rocco Cronglisto
Carl Sinisgalli
Douglas Cresent
Tony Rotundo

Tony studied the names . . . and by God . . . Carlo was on the money. Tony himself had forgot some of the names and faces but the list . . . and . . . another peek at the old photo brought most of it back.

It was another time and another place . . .
God Bless East Utica!!!
God Bless *that* East Utica!!!

A Thousand Words . . . Ash Wednesday

Tony held the photo by pinching the lower left hand corner; he did not want to leave finger prints on the glossy finish. It was a very old photo. His mother kept this and many others in an old shoe box. As he studied it, he absent mindedly started snapping his fingers with his right hand. An old habit, which he often did when concentrating.

Tony once told his oldest son, "A picture is worth a thousand words."

In a heartbeat, his son replied, "Oh Yeah?? Show me a picture of the Gettysburg Address." Tony still smiles when ever he recalls that smart-ass response.

A thousand words??? A snap shot taken by a Kodak box camera a zillion years ago??? Whaddaya think??? Tony thought:

Page down

"That's Jimmy Moore standing next to me . . . the only colored kid in the class . . . later there'd be more . . . a lot more. I liked Jimmy . . . he was a good kid . . . last time I saw him was at the St. Rosalie Feast by Mount Carmel Church . . . right after I got out of the army. I was going with that Sicilian girl. Funny, when I introduced him to her . . . I sensed he (for some reason or other) was hesitant in shaking her hand. I think he finally did so reluctantly. He kind of smiled and looked away and it reminded me of Paulie and his bashful ways . . .

A couple of years later . . . one of my nieces told me of an incident. I think she was working at a bank or something . . . she had a desk in a very large work area.

Along with other things, her desk top contained a transcribing machine, her name plate and a telephone. She was experiencing difficulties with the transcribing machine and the bank requested a service call. With in a week, a Pitney-Bowes or maybe a Monroe Calculator representative/service person stopped at her desk.

He was a well dressed, well mannered black man. Although not required, he politely introduced himself and asked permission to examine the equipment.

As he started to work, his eye caught my niece's name plate. He recognized the surname and asked if she was related to me. They struck up a short but pleasant conversation. When my niece told me about the meeting, her eyes widen slightly and in her teenage girlish voice, told me how well dressed and how handsome and how well mannered, this Mr. James Moore was.

Atta boy Jim!!!! Ya did all right!!! Pitney-Bowes . . . or . . . Monroe Recording . . . what ever . . . shirt and tie . . . a real Sidney Poitier . . . I'm happy for you guy!!!

I always liked Jimmy!! He was a good kid!!!

That's Jack Del Monte giving a salute . . . actually he was probably shading his eyes from the November sun. Jack died young . . . the kid was strong . . . smart . . . a natural leader . . . in my opinion anyway. We went into the army at the same time and within two years he made sergeant . . . and he later opened up a joint on Route 5 somewhere. Last time I saw him he was almost as wide as he was tall . . . full mustache . . . bald . . . still quick to smile. Was it the twenty-fifth re-union?? He used to live in the John Blaze brownstone at the corner of Catherine and Pellettieri.

Those two kids squatting way over at the end on the left side are Sebastiano Convertino and Pasqual Caputo. They did well. Buster Convertino got into politics for a while and even ran for mayor and Pat became an opera singer. Buster was always a good looking kid: he had greenish-blue eyes, a rarity in the neighborhood, and he was smart, very smart. My mother always like 'Sebastiano' because when ever they'd run into one another he would always ask about her well being and ask about me. I saw Buster at my bother's funeral/wake . . . still good looking.

Pat could not be more Italian if he had been born in the Old Country. He was the epitome of the culture we were all proud of. He started the violin in the first grade later piano . . . grew up with his grandmother in Joe Salerno's house . . . a frame two story structure between Jack Del Monte's brownstone and mine. He loved music, loved the Italian language: he spoke the 'pure', not the bastardized version most of the other guys use. He could not be anymore Italian, had he been raised/nursed by a she wolf in the Apennine Mountains of Italy. As a matter of fact, he signed my year book in Italian . . . wishing me Buono Fortuno per tutti la vita . . . or something like that. That might have been the last time I saw him . . . I wonder if he'd remember me today?

The two guys next to Pat are Joe Graziano and Vinny Scalzo. They are both dead. Joe, I understand, found his way up to Maine. He owned and operated a very successful restaurant up there someplace. He used to live on Elizabeth Street . . . a good kid. I don't remember Vinny graduating from Brandegee; maybe he transferred. Mount Carmel had a parochial school, but I just don't remember.

Later in life, Vinny befriended one of my cousins and they became pretty good buddies. I was told he died an accidental death while moving furniture somewhere. I cringe when I think of the cause and how he died. He had a twin . . . his name was Salvatore . . . but I don't remember him being in any of my classes.

Look at that skinny Carlo!!! On the left of that towhead . . . Carl became a Brownie for the Department of Transportation. Back in the early to mid sixties, when my wife went for her driving test, it was Carl who conducted the road test. I remember, Carl had my wife sign something, got out of the car, nodded a quick hello to me on his way to the next road test, and as he passed me, in sotto voce said, "She did okay." Guess they weren't suppose to fraternize.

There's Tony Rotundo on the right hand side of the tow head kid. Who the hell is he?? Can't place him or remember him. Ya think I could. . . . I brag about my good memory all the time.

Yeah . . . Tony Rotundo of course! Kind of quiet kid, had a fist full of sisters. My cousin, Sam I think, dated one of them, and as I recall it was 'serious' as we used to say. Sam ended up marrying a nice girl from down around of St. Anthony Street. Tony Rotundo had an older sister that was a real knock out.

Whenever I see or remember Tony, I can't help but think of grape crates.

I remember one time Mrs. Utter (second grade), wanted to teach the class a little bit about banking. What she really wanted was to promote the sales of *saving stamps* and encourage war time savings and buying war bonds for the war effort. The class decided if we could get three wooden grape boxes, place two on the ground in a upright position, separate them slightly, and in this space join the boxes at the top . . . maybe we could . . .

Page Down

Tony continued to muse,

"A thousand words . . . You are right Peter . . . I can't do it in a thousand words. Who the hell could? Looking at this photo there's a zillion words left to be said . . . there's George Frattassio . . . (I understand he pretty sick now) . . . there's a life time to tell about him . . . and Skip Lisandrelli. I once dated his wife's sister. Skip went to "Sister School" at Our Lady of Mount Carmel and then to Utica Catholic Academy. I think he played some basketball there . . . as a matter of fact . . . if memory serves me correctly, he went to the University of Notre Dame. Atta boy, Skip! Good job!

Look at those faces staring at you from the past . . . whadda ya gonna say to them?? Whadda are they trying to tell you??? Listen!!! Try to understand . . . if you can!

Tony recalled an Ash Wednesday years back. He had an overnighter in Wilkes-Barre, Pennsylvania. He got up especially early because he wanted to attend Mass and get the 'ashes'. There is an old parish up in the Hill District . . . predominately Polish . . . predominately blue collar. It had an un-scheduled special 6:00AM Mass to accommodate the devout parishioners . . . factory workers. More than eighty per-cent of the attendees were women, and Tony also noted that the men who had lunch pails, placed them on the floor, near the kneelers, and not on the pews. Humble people . . . good people.

After the Mass, the padre went to the center of the communion/altar railing: two altar boys dutifully open the gate. The parishioners obediently arose, formed two rows and slowly made their way up to the main altar.

Working people, men with large strong callused hands, women with bauskas (kerchiefs) over their head . . . all made their way to the altar of God . . . God the joy of my youth. The women would return home later that day in the afternoon . . . many with lint in their hair. The men would return with empty lunch pails, some still hungry.

Tony joined the procession up to the main altar. The priest, the black-as-sin-ashes, the stockade shuffle to the altar gate, reminded him that this life is not forever. As he neared the open altar gate, the litany and repetitive priest's words drifted back to him. It increased ever so slightly as he neared the tray of black ashes.

Remember man that you are dust and to dust you shall return.

It was said to each and every person, on the right and on the left, who had ashes placed on their foreheads. A sing-song cadence, softly and quietly said . . . that immersed it's meaning in to the depth of your soul. The works were now in English . . . in the real old days, Tony remembered that it was said in Latin.

The parishioners would cross themselves, turn and leave the communion railing gate. Tony, even with his tie and shirt and blue suit and black oxford shoes did the same thing. He didn't look like he belonged among those holy and hard working people, but *HIS God* knew him and understood him. (At least that was what Tony wished for.)

Tony left the church and it was still dark out . . . Easter came early that year, but as he walked away, he could still hear . . . *and to dust thou shall return.*

Intro to Paulie

Page Up

The first time Tony remembers seeing Paulie was his first day in the fifth grade at Brandegee School. Tony's class has just been promoted from the fourth grade (Ms. Baker's class) and moved en masse, single file—boy girl boy—into the dreaded room 14 (Ms. Bailey's pivotal fifth grade). "*If'n* ya can get through *dat* grade, ya can go right to college, especially with Ms. Bailey teaching!"

Ms. Bailey was standing at her desk, about a zillion feet tall under the flag, not smiling. The wall behind her had a long slate blackboard running horizontally from one corner to the next: three and a half feet from the floor and five and a half feet from the ceiling.

She gave a directional signal with her right arm and hand, pointing to the door that the kids entered, and swung her arm around the three walls of the classroom. Room 14 was a corner room, well-lit with windows on the east and south sides. The first to enter got the message and dutifully obeyed by going to the rear of the room past the cloakroom behind the stationary desks under the window walls and eventually formed a *U* in front of the tall lady with slightly bucked teeth, standing under the flag with a stern look on her face.

They quietly marched in, still single file, some of them darting a quick look at that tall, tall lady. (Betcha *ma* head wouldn't even reach her shoulder, maybe!) Then Tony thought, *she ain't as round as Ma or Zia, neither!*

Her first words to the new class were "No talking!" and then she growled around the recently formed "U." "Yeah! Like ya *hadda* say *dat*!" The girls in the class—many with brand-new dresses for the first day of school, four still in pigtails—hugged their notebook tighter and pulled in their necks, some not even blinking! Maybe that notebook pressed to their breast, like a chastity belt over the heart, would protect them.

Few of the boys ever hugged their books like the girls did but carried them rakishly by their hips. Truth be known, more than half of them were as frightened and/or terrorized as the girls were of this tall stern lady. Tony thought, *Holy cow! What da other guys said 'bout her gotta be true!*

"All right," she said, "I am going to assign you your desk. When you leave your desk in the future, you are to go to the left and down the aisle; the left for those of you who don't know the difference is the side toward the windows over there!!" She pointed to the south side of the room. Those kids on the L side of the room looked at the windows; those in front of the windows turned around to make sure they (the windows) were there.

She sat at her desk and opened the middle drawer and pulled out a large piece of white cardboard with a grid on it. It contained the plot and the seating plan. "Listen closely, people! When your name is called, you are to go to the desk I assign to you. Should either the desk or seat be too high or too low, get into it anyway for the time being. Mr. Lux (who was one of the custodians) will be here before ten o'clock and make all necessary adjustments."

A silence followed, then "Josephine Albiano!" Josephine released her right arm from the death grip it had on her books clutched to her breast, raised it, and said in a weak, girlish voice, "Here, Ms. Bailey."

"First roll, front seat . . . over there." She pointed. She referred to her chart and was about to call the next name, when Mrs. Wilson, Mr. Hixon's secretary, appeared in the doorway. She entered the classroom, followed by a kind of tall boy who hugged his books like a girl. Ms. Bailey did not get up from her seat; she was a Cortland Normal State graduate and Ms. Wilson was—who knows?—certainly not a college graduate.

"Yes?" she said.

Mrs. Wilson came over to her desk under the flag, bent over slightly and whispered quietly into her ear, as she handed her a folder. Ms. Bailey frowned, looked at her chart again, and said something to Mrs. Wilson. Only Josephine and some of the kids closer to the Ms. Bailey's desk heard the response.

"Well, why wasn't I told before?" she asked indignantly. Poor Mrs. Wilson only shrugged her shoulders. Ms. Bailey, with a certain amount of disdain and annoyance, went back to her chart and studied the seating arrangements. Then she said to Mrs. Wilson, "Oh! All right, let him stand over there (the spot that Josephine just vacated)!" Mrs. Wilson just sort of half nodded and turned to leave as she did. She caught the eye of the boy she just escorted in, smiled warmly, and left the room. The boy stepped up to the vacancy and waited, still hugging his books.

Ms. Bailey partially opened her middle-desk drawer, just enough so that she could pick up a pink rubber pencil eraser out of a tray and erase a name from one of the squares. She quickly jerked her head up and looked around the *U* to make sure no one was talking or whatever. She then picked up the chart, tipped it toward the nearby waste basket, and brushed off the spent erasure.

Years of experience had taught her that whenever she made up a seating plan, she had to leave at least two vacant desks at the end of each row of school desks. Last year she got three colored kids assigned to her class, two girls and a boy, from a migrant camp in the middle of October—October for God's sake! Even after the picking season was over, at least one of those families never went back to Georgia. She was pretty sure she saw one of them in the halls this morning.

Oh, well, she thought, *back to the seating assignments.* She said, "The boy who did not get promoted, what's his name? Let's see . . . Paul . . . he'll go in front of that large curly haired boy, Anthony." She took the occasion to look at both Paul and then Tony. She made a quick mental evaluation; *one will probably be a truck driver, the other just another factor worker or a floor sweeper.* She then mentally noted, *what a coincidence! Their surnames werein alphabetically sequenced.* She said, "Well, boys, if you stay together for the next three years here at Brandegee you are going to be close neighbors in the classroom."

"Angela Belliano?",she called out.

"Here, Mrs. Bailey!" Angela answered; and like what Josephine did before her; she raised her right hand and with her left arm clutched her books even closer to her bosom.

"Over there behind Josephine," Ms. Bailey said. Angela quickly obeyed. Ms. Bailey then made a mental evaluation of her: *Bright shining eyes, nicely dressed, well-groomed hair, quick and obedient, new shoes; if she reads well and understands math, maybe college, at least a secretarial position, not just another factory girl.*

And so it went: everyone was eventually seated. Paul and Tony needed adjustment to their permanent desk—Tony much more so than Paul. Only Big Jumbo Pat and Junior Del Monte were a little bit bigger than Tony. They squirmed as they waited for the appearance of Mr. Lux, with those two special wrenches: one for the desk (which, like the seat, were anchored to the floor) and the other for the seat. Sometimes he had to use both. The custodian arrived.

Ms. Bailey arose and walked down the first aisle. Mr. Lux, with his two wrenches, quietly followed her. She, and certainly not anyone of her students, was going to tell Mr. Lux which desk or chair needed an adjustment. It was form of control and power.

She was now well ahead of the custodian who was lowering a desk for a girl way up front. Ms. Bailey's inspection consisted of looking to see how close the knees were to the bottom of the desk and also checking to see if the students' knees, thighs, and hips formed a straight line.

If she deemed it necessary, she would tell the student to stand and wait for Mr. Lux. It was a slow process. Mr. Lux would loosen either the two bolts on the desk or the one on the seat and make the adjustment. In the final test, he'd ask the student to sit, make a fist, and put his fist on his knees; this procedure supposedly allowed for future growth over the next nine months.

When Ms. Bailey got to Paul's desk, she cocked her head slightly, checked his legs, and told him to stand. She only glanced at Tony and merely said, "Up!" A relieved Tony lumbered up and out of a very uncomfortable desk. As she walked away, she realized that two boys standing on the aisle as the custodian tried to work was not practical and ordered the boys to go stand by the window until Mr. Lux called them. Paul and Tony stood side by side and silently watched Ms. Bailey continue down the rows, inspecting.

When she was out of whisper range, Tony whispered out of the side of his mouth, "What's your name kid?" He had missed when Ms. Bailey called it and assigned him his desk. Paul's eyes widened, a look of terror crossed his face, and thought, *Didn't this guy know there is no talking in Ms. Bailey's class?*

Tony saw the look but didn't understand why. He said again in that "out of the side of your mouth" whisper, "*Whatcha* name?" Paul looked away. He still had that panic look on his face like somebody was going to kill both of them in the back of the room under the windows while they waited for Mr. Lux. Ms. Bailey was as far as she could get. Tony shot a quick look in her direction, found it safe, and asked for the third time, "*Whatcha* name?"

"Paul," he whispered softly.

He said it so low that Tony missed it. Tony said, "What?"

"Paul!" he repeated a little bit louder and then added,

"I don't wanna get in trouble."

Tony smirked and was about to answer when the custodian said, "Who is sitting here?" Paul nervously stepped forward without an oral reply. Mr. Lux said to him, "Sit down, son, make two fists and put them on your knees. That's it, good boy, how does that feel?" Paul just nodded his approval, dared not even to speak to an adult. Few, if any, ever spoke kindly to Paul, let alone call him "son."

Page Down

Tony lit up one of those Tuscany cigars he got the last time he was "home." It was Sunday, and he and his sons were out on the back patio/porch. Tony was talking about the last time he went to Utica. He was telling them about sitting in a picnic pavilion, talking to some of the old Brandegee boys—Guy, who now wants to be called Gaetano, Carlo, and Big Jumbo Pat's younger brother Carmen—with a cold pitcher of beer on the picnic table and large Styrofoam cups. They were just *talkin' 'bout the old days.*

"'Member, they used to spread the cinders on the school grounds instead of planting grass?"

"How 'bout the time Frankie pushed Jap and Jap fell, broke his glasses, and scratched the shit out of his arms?"

"'Member waiting for the janitors to open the school doors on those cold February mornings?"

"Talk about *'s not* those kids!"

"Do ya 'member when Paulie tripped and fell in front of . . ."

Before Tony could finish, Carlo said, "He died, you know?"

"What?" Tony asked and exclaimed, "Incredible . . . !" "What?" he repeated.

"Yeah!" chimed in Carlo and Gaetano.

"When? How?" Tony asked the questions, but the replies really didn't register. His mouth dropped open, his eyes got a little watery (he hoped no one noticed; he looked away), and he felt a deep sadness. *Dat's not important! When and how*, he thought. *Oh! Shit! I hadda tell Paulie a thousand things! Stuff like I was sorry for always being a wannabe, wanna be a star, wanted the broads to fall all over me, and not being a good friend to you like you were to me . . . All you wanted Paulie, was just to be my friend, and I let you down. I wasn't your friend all the time . . . just when it was convenient for me . . . and now it's too late to make it up . . . if I ever can! Oh! Shit!* Tony crossed himself, uttering, "In the name of the Father and of the Son and the Holy Ghost . . . yeah, still the Holy Ghost . . . because that was the way he was taught."

He told his sons how he met Paulie. He went on to describe him: a little bit taller than most, drooled a lot, always pulling out a handkerchief from his back pocket to wipe his mouth, probably just the opposite of a kid you see on TV, pitching computer games; no bright eyes, sandy hair, full smile showing perfect teeth; kid, no! Just a kid (and hating to say it aloud even after all these years) just a kid who was a little slow. The story was he fell out of a window when he was a kid and took a good rap on his head. He had all kinds of trouble with arithmetic—big time!—but everything else, he was as good as Tony, better sometimes.

Sure, for a time he carried his books and ran like a girl and threw a ball like a girl; but everything else, he was okay. Tony's brother Angelo told him, "Paulie had an older brother too, and this kid was a brain—he went to RPI. Guess, maybe once, Paulie had natural potential . . . but an accident dealt him a bad hand to play."

"*Ah nutter ding,*" Tony continued, "Paulie was very shy, never made eye contact; he'd talk to ya and he would be lookin' at the top of your shoulder or down at the ground behind your knee; you knew he had to force himself to raise his eyes and look ya in the face and a second later, back they'd go to the looking at the ground and him finishing what he was saying. And he was soft-spoken too! I never ever heard him yell. *Lotta* guys used to tease him . . . me too! What an asshole I must have been at times; but I guess kids, all kids, aren't really . . . What? Sensitive? . . . Ahh! Kids are kids!"

Tony suddenly remembered a time when it was just he and Paulie walking home from Proctor. In the summer time or early spring or fall, Paul would go down Mohawk Street (north), go through some alleyways of the textile mills, cross eight sets of New York Central railroad tracks, climb a short dike/ramp, and go to the wetlands near the Barge Canal and the Mohawk River. He did that alone because he didn't have too many friends. It was quiet there and he could look at "life," and nobody would be judging him. He'd look for hawks and white pigeons and occasionally a flock of geese flying in a V formation. It made him feel good—a nice warm feeling.

Tony recalled that walk home with Paulie that afternoon because it was probably the first and only time that Paulie ever really opened up to him. Funny how one remembers something like that a lifetime later, but memories like that come always back to him. He told Tony that the Saturday before he went down to the wetlands and watched a flock of geese fly overhead and later watched three hawks circle slowly and effortlessly, wings expanded to maximum, gliding, defining gravity—pretty majestic. The hawks would be looking for pigeons or rabbits or fi eld mice. Then he told Tony about the geese honking and beating their wings to move forward, following the outside wing of the bird to its front, honking, maybe to encourage the others, maybe fearing gravity.

Tony listened, fascinated by Paulie's description. Then Paulie said to him, "Maybe I'm like those geese. I gotta work hard just to stay in place and not fall out of formation." Tony didn't reply or make any comment to Paulie's observation. Tony just looked at him, and Paulie shot a glance at Tony and then quickly looked down at the sidewalk and remained silent; and they continued their walk home. Tony turned right on Kossuth, and Paulie continued on to Albany down to Bleecker, Mohawk, and then to the brownstone on the southwest corner of Jay and Mohawk.

"Aw, Paulie, Paulie, Paulie, what makes you think you are the only one who has to beat your wings, who has to struggle to stay up, who lacks a Midas touch? That's what I would tell him today!" But Tony knew, if he did, Paulie would only look at a spot on the ground.

"But I do remember one time," Tony continued telling his sons, "that he looked me straight in the eye and held the look . . . once I said to him, '*Whaddar* ya, Paulie, Lebanese or Syrian?' His eyes shot up and he looked me squarely in the eye and . . . 'I'm Armenian!' . . . like he took it as an insult that I should think he was something other than Armenian. He scolded me with that look. I still remember the 'look' . . . a hundred years later!" Tony shook his head and became silent and looked at nothing special other than an orange ashtray. He flicked his cigar ashes into it and thought, *Oh shit! Now he is dead.*

Page Up

Paulie and his mother, she leaning against the hallway wall by the auditorium entrance at Brandegee School, the eighth-grade graduating class of nineteen, whatever; but whenever that scene/memory crossed Tony's mind, he felt a melancholy feeling—a kind of sorrow deep within him. Tony had two aunts, and three cousins came to see him when he graduated that afternoon (the men were working), and there was going to be a party for him when he would get home.

Shit! He knew that Paul would not have a party or anything like that. He only had one older brother, and his father died a long time ago. It damped Tony's spirit. He pushed it out of his mind, but it came back at different times, for a long time. Even now, he'll occasionally see that image/scene of mother and son standing alone by the auditorium door, nothing to say to each other, quietly looking around. Tony and a couple of friends would walk up Kossuth Avenue to Albany Street then up Albany to Hilton Avenue and hang a right and then hike to Thomas R. Proctor High School, the last leg. Paulie's route was up Mohawk, a short, quick half block on Bleecker to Albany Street; and the long stretch to Hilton Avenue was okay whenhe could use Paulie—to copy his homework or do him favors.

"Paulie, take my books, will ya, and put them on my desk. I gotta take a piss . . . if the bell rings and if Mrs. Maycook says something, tell her I'll be right there," Tony requested. Paulie's homework was always neat and concise, a very legible, easy-to-read handwriting, maybe not as elaborated and/or fl owing as the Palmer Method System (oval—oval—push pull—push pull) but a heck of a lot better than Tony's handwriting; with time, Tony's handwriting worsened. It got *worst*!

Carmen's . . . and Espresso

Page Down

It was the same morning that Tony found out about Fridone. He was going to go home and wanted to pick up some cannoli's and maybe some pusties, the kids and the wife loved the cannoli, so he stopped at Carmen's. He could have stopped at the Florentine, but for some reason . . . maybe the loneliness in his heart . . . that feeling that a loss was forever . . . and eternal . . . Edgar Allen Poe's '. . . quote the raven, nevermore.' A little old man . . . drunk . . . sleeping in a snow bank . . . freezing his fingers off. Tony needed to see old familiar faces.

Maybe old Carmen would be there . . . he went to school with Tony's older bothers . . . Angelo and Salvatore . . . and over the years became a good friend of the family. His daughter now runs the little pastacerria . . . but he still comes around to help out.

Maybe some of the guys would be there having espresso. Years ago Carmen purchase a magnificent coffee espresso machine . . . shinny brass fixtures and urns . . . a giant urn . . . front and center . . . with a cupola . . . more than two feet . . . standing at attention . . . propped up on a countertop . . . so wide and handsome . . . it demanded your un-divided attention when you walked into the café. Beautiful . . . just beautiful!!! Did someone once tell Tony that Carmen did not get it from Italy, but from San Francisco . . . he wasn't sure.

Tony walked in . . . the sight of the espresso machine . . . and three big men sitting at one of the small circular tables . . . with little demitasse cups . . . and little spoons resting in saucers . . . and Carmen leaning on the display counter . . . that black mood vanished. God Bless East Utica!!! It lives.

Tony was loudly greeted and welcomed not only by Carmen, but two of the three large men at the small circular table. Out from under that black mood, Tony had . . . almost instantaneously become . . . robust . . . jolly . . . delighted . . . glad to be alive!! After a series of the quick . . . *"How r yooze??"* Tony still standing, pointed to the lower portion of the double glass door upright refrigerator cooler (used mainly to display various pastries) where Carmen stored the green liter bottles of Pellegrino mineral water and in a high pitch, nasal sound voice (Tony's best imitation of an English accent) told Carmen, "Would you be so kind, my good man, to pick out the finest Pellegrino bottle . . . vintage 1948 please . . . and bring it to this table along with four glasses . . . for me and my friends to partake . . . and . . . I must see the cork!! I insist!!!" He then sat with the three men . . . at a much too small circular table.

They exchanged greetings again, and Tony was introduced to the un-known person. A kid from Little Falls, who is Italian (third generation) and was a biology professor at Utica College.

It was an old routine he and Carmen had developed over the years. And Carmen, with the loaded tray in hand, a large neatly folded napkin draped over his forearm, served the table. Ceremoniously he unscrewed the cap off of the green bottle, pompously placed it in front of Tony, took a glass, poured just enough to cover the bottom, and handed it Tony. Tony stuck his nose into glass . . . inhaled deeply . . . then lifted the glass to the light to check the liquid for clarity . . . sipped a little bit . . . sealing his lips immediately . . . swished the liquid in his mouth . . . under the tongue . . . on his gums . . . then noisily popped his lips opened. He picked up the metal screw cap, sniffed it, examining it for color, and then place the 'cork' back on the table.

Carmen stood (sober and stoic) by the table, napkin still draped over forearm, holding the green bottle, and watching Tony's face. Tony gave him a quick nod, then one of the best pastry makers in East Utica, humbly poured out the mineral water for the seated men. The others at the table were delighted and awed by the performance.

"I don't know which of us is the better actor . . . you or me," Tony said.

"It's gotta be you, fat ass, I am only a waiter."

"Hey Carmen a little respect . . . besides . . . I haven't paid you yet!!!" and then Tony added, "gimme a cup of espresso and a biscotti . . . one of those almond ones . . . okay?"

Carmen made a fist with his thumb straight out, and kind of jerked it downward. "Sure . . . what da hell da ya tink??? I'm an orphan or sumptin??"

The little hand gesture was a signal. Carmen went to the magnificent coffee machine and made Tony his espresso. The young girl working the pastry counter, put Tony's almond biscotti on a small serving dish and delivered it to the small table. Tony noticed she had a clear plastic glove on left hand. "It wasn't always like that, hope the biscotti still taste as good . . . it will", Tony thought.

When Carmen finished making Tony's coffee, both he and the demitasse coffee cup disappeared into the back room, but quickly returned. Tony sipped his coffee and it had a rich anise flavor. He smiled and nodded to Carmen.

Carmen pulled up a nearby chair and flopped down into it. When you get older it is always good to sit down among friends and friends of friends. *Le amici e'amici di amici.* He soon joined in on the pinball type conversation that was going on . . . most of it about the old days. "Carm, ya remember Santo Ferraro's store and steam ship ticket agency? Don't you?? You grew up down there around Wetmore School didn't ya??"

"Of course I do!!"

"We were just talking bout when we used to mail bundles/packages to the old country . . . we use to take them there to his ticket agency . . . he also ran a grocery import store . . . remember?? He must have been a smart guy to get that steamship ticket agency contract and . . . ."

Carm interrupted the speaker by saying, "He wasn't the brains in that operation, his wife was!!" He should know . . . he grew down there around St. Anthony's Church.

They . . . Bob, Carmen and Tony . . . remembered the hand sewn pillow cases and the old clothes line used to wrap them. The other two . . . the kid from Little Falls . . . who was much too young . . . if he was even born . . . and Big Ray who was Armenian . . . listen with child like curiosity and wonderment.

Bob chimed in. He had studied art in Italy and told a story about something that happened to him there. As a youngster . . . and future artist . . . he had a steady and concise hand . . . his lettering was neat and legible. This talent earned him the responsibility to address those hand sewn pillow cases and clothes line-tied package to the family in the old country. A very big thing for a youngster.

Years later, after high school . . . military experience . . . college . . . and a warehouse loft studio in Roma . . . (not too far from Keat's Spanish Steps) . . . Bob took an opportunity to go visit one of his ancient aunts. He relished the excitement and the thrill of the occasion. It brought him to a humble peasant farm house high in the mountains east of Naples and Rome. He was treated like royalty. They could not do enough for him . . . they did all that they could for him . . . within their power and limits.

Soon the time came for Bob to return to Rome. That morning, they made a simple breakfast for him and after, he and his elderly uncle and two male cousins sat by the hearth finishing the coffee and talking about America.

Other than his ancient aunt, the only other female present was her granddaughter. A sixteen-seventeen year old beauty . . . a natural beauty. She wore her hair in a bun and always wore a certain set of gold earrings, an old gift from her Godfather—uncle in America The women had washed Bob's white shirt. The one he was going to wear that day for the trip back to Rome.

They insisted on ironing it. He protested saying it was too much bother and not really necessary. Neither she nor her grandmother could bear the thought of their American artist relative going to the ferrovia (iron way . . . railroad) wearing a beautiful white shirt that wasn't properly pressed. Never!!!

He sipped his coffee . . . made small talk with his cousins and watched that beautiful Italian girl with a saintly profile, perfectly almond shaped eyes . . . he never had seen such dark sparkling eyes like that!! The women working together cleared the kitchen table and prepping it to be used as an ironing board. The beauty placed two heavy cast iron boat shaped ironing pieces near the fire in the hearth. The unit that would contain/control and steer those heavy cast iron pieces was taken out of the 'steebee' (cupboard) and placed nearby, but not too near the hearth. The holder did not have to be hot . . . for that matter . . . the grip attached to the top of the unit was made of wood.

Bob realized he was staring . . . almost gawking at the siren . . . he quickly looked away from the hearth and tried to pick up on the conversations his uncle and cousins were engaged in. He felt embarrassed . . . almost ashamed (. . . she's only a kid for Christ-sake!! ya jerk!!! Whaddaya doin??

For Christ sakes!! She's only seventeen !! Jesus . . . I must be nuts!!) . . . he fired off a question about figs trees . . . maybe a little too loud . . . he had hoped not. Bob sipped his coffee and told his audience how . . . in America . . . in Utica . . . you either wrapped your fig trees or buried them for the winter.

"Ahh!!!" they chimed in unison, "Interno e' lo freddo!!!" (The winter and the cold) and nodding and smiling and praising the ingenuity and wisdom of their countrymen in far off Utica.

Just then, something happened that saved him . . . and . . . made the awkwardness of the moment vanish. His elderly aunt had completed placing a neatly folded woolen blanket on the kitchen table which was soon to be used as an ironing board. She went to cupboard and retrieved what appeared to be a towel or a sheet of some kind.

Bob had been balancing the fragile demitasse saucer in his left hand and occasionally picking up the small cup by its gold painted ear and took little sips. He was about to do it again when . . . he suddenly stopped . . . in mid air so to say . . . his jaw dropped open. Quickly and carefully he returned the cup to the saucer and arose and started for the table. His aunt had returned to the table, unfolded the towel/clothe she had just retrieved, snapped it to make it wrinkle free . . . it seemed to floated momentarily like a sail . . . that had just caught the first motion of a light breeze. It came to rest neatly and easily upon the coarse blanket . . . the ironing board was now ready.

Bob neared the table and with a slight hand gestured, froze both women from commencing their self-delegated task. The white protective cloth, was an old pillow case, and it had writing on it . . . done in indelible ink . . . which was placed thereon by a kid . . . with a very steady hand . . . that was in the seventh grade at Conkling Elementary School in Utica and, who was now there looking down at it after many years, Bob explained. He looked at the young blossoming beauty and thought. "Yeah!! and probably before you were even born".

That imagine of a beautiful young virgin with little circular gold ear rings and an old pillow case with evidence of his earlier consecrated, steady and neat art work and a wrinkled old woman looking straight into his eyes, would remain forever in his memory bank.

"Ayya!!" the elderly aunt said after hearing about his involvement with the pillow case, "Everyone and every thing has value and worth." (So you tell me! What is junk??)

Tony then took center stage and related an incident (on the similar subject) that occurred recently when he visited the old country with his son. They were dinner guests at one of his second cousin's home (on his mother's side) and the woman went out of her way to provide a feast . . . an abundonza!!! Her pregnant daughter (six months) helped as best she could, as did her siblings and aunts and female cousins. They all rendered valuable assistance to the hostess, setting the table, being active and participating guests at the meal, clearing the table, telling stories, asking questions: they as much as their male counterparts enjoyed the festivities. (Maybe more so . . . like the Gospel reminds us . . . he (she) who serves is the greatest among you.)

Tony sat to the right of the hostess's husband (who was soon to . . . within three years to retire from banking in far off Milan) at a table that was covered with good food and wines . . . and . . . surrounded by family. The host was so very proud of his wife, you only had to look at him when he looked at her to know how true that was.

After the numerous courses of meats and fish and pasta . . . the table was cleared by the 'youngster' but vigilantly supervised by Tony's second cousin, a very large bowl of fruits and a bowl of nuts was placed in the center of the table. Everyone lamented . . . no one had anymore room left to eat . . . not even the tiniest mouthful.

La maganetta (the coffee pot/machine) was placed on the table upon a potholder. Bottles of strega and anisette and grappa, now stood tall with empty (and soon to be empty) bottles of white and red wine. A tray filled with bluish Murano cordial glasses were brought to the table and placed in front of the host, near the cordials and grappa.

When all were seated again at . . . (or what Tony was eventually to remember as an altar of family and food . . .) the dining room table, the host asked the hostess what after dinner cordial she would prefer. She was seated at the opposite end, blushed slightly and protested that the guest of honor should be first—neither Tony nor her husband would hear it: tonight she was to be honored with first drink off of the "boss's tray." She softly said, "un poco de anisette, grazia" (A little anisette, thank you.)

Tony and his son and all the guests sent up a cheer of "Bravo!!", clapped their hands and she blushed again. Her husband carefully handed the partially filled cordial glass to Tony who, beaming with delight, careful passes it to his neighbor who in turn did the same, and so on until that small chalice that containing a half ounce of anisette arrived. When she took it, another cheer went up and everyone was thanking her and wishing her well, she smiled slowly, lowered her head slightly to the left, accepted the praise silently and then raised her cordial glass slightly toward the opposite end of the table and her husband.

Husband and wife smiled at one another as if they were the only ones in the room. Tony caught the tenderness of the gesture and thought it was one of the most loving things he had ever seen.

The host then asked Tony what his pleasure was: obliged him, and then continued to serve the others. The evening mellowed. All stomachs were filled. Nut shells, banana and orange peels seem to gather in little plates at various spots on the table; sharing space with all the various bottles, and someone recounted an incident . . . a story. Then some else, then another, and another, old stories and new stories; being recalled and recounted to the family audience. The type of stories that are the cement of memories and the longevity of history. You hold them, and keep them in your thoughts . . . forever!

The subject at the table turned to the relief bundles and packages during the late forties that Tony's mom and aunts used to send to Italy. His brother, Salvatore's Nehru sport jacket for zio Caesario, (he was smart and was to go to the 'universita' in Pescara soon), wool socks, a pair of shoes that would fit 'someone', girls dresses, boys shirts, a home made cotton cloth bag (fabricated from scraps from the textile mill and snuck home in a lunch pail) filled with used and various size buttons and a couple spools of thread and some sewing needles.

Tony could remember one time, long ago when his mother received a letter from her oldest sister Caesario's mother . . . and as she and Zia Grazia and Zia Lucia sat at her kitchen table . . . in far away Utica, she read the letter aloud. It advised them that they had received three bundles since Christmas and were ecstatic and overjoyed with them. Tony's Zia Maria Nicola thanked his mother and aunts profusely she blessed the milk that nursed all of them. Zia Maria Nicola continued and told them that the buttons and thread and needles were God sent. She had a thousand uses for them, so practical, so valuable.

Those strong stout Mediterranean women sitting at a kitchen table, in far away East Utica, did a strange thing then that Tony will remember till the day he dies. When Tony's ma read the complimentary part about the buttons, she burst out in tears. As if on cue, her sisters followed in a heart beat, tears running from their eyes. Their noses started running, they squeezed their eyes shut and blindly reached for the home made handkerchiefs they had in their apron pocket. After a moment or two, the tears subsided. They took deep breaths and composed themselves once more.

But to think !!! Their saintly Maria Nicola, matriarch of the family—she who had to remain in Italy to tend to their aging father (he was denied entry at Ellis Island in 1913) and raise eleven kids, had two sons serve in North Africa, four daughters who eventually became nuns, another son die of TB shortly after the war—*all this!!!*—and—this brave, strong woman—who suffered so much—was thanking her younger sisters for what?? Nothing! Junk! A small sack of used mostly un-matched buttons, some lousy spools of thread, an a couple little needles!

It was too much!!! (Troppo!! Troppo!!) Tony's mother was the first to again burst out tears. The sisters followed instantaneously. Only this time they stood and hugged one another.

The hostess too, remembered those bundles from Santo Ferrarro's steamship ticket agency and deep down in East Utica. As a little girl she best remembered the bundles from Zia Lucia and Zia Grazia, who had daughters, thus guaranteeing some used pretty dresses or girlish things.

She would, however, best remember sitting at her grandmother's table and watching her open one of the bundles. It was probably like Christmas for all the kids, hoping. There were the usual oohs and aahs as the bundle's contents were revealed and, sometimes found tucked in a pocket somewhere would be *(Lo and Behold)* a pack of chewing gum.

She even remembered the brand name of the gum and the coloring of the packet . . . Black Jack . . . blue and white and black wrapping. Her brother Filippo, who was sitting directly across from Tony remembered and reminded some of those who were present at the bundle openings how his grand parents made him a practical pair of suspenders. They worked great and he used them for years afterward. Filippo is now a gymnasium (high school) math teacher and does some tutoring.

He told Tony how his grand parents made those not so elegant suspenders for him. His grandfather, Tony's Zio Filippo, would first carefully and neatly punch four holes in the waist band of his trousers; two in the front and two in the rear. His grandmother would securely sow a small metal washer over each of the punctures to the waist band. The clothes line rope that was used on the package/bundle, was cut in two, knotted at two thirds it's length (the knot for the rear), measured to fit over the boys shoulders and then tied it to the waist line metal washer attachments.

Filippo told Tony, they always held. He really didn't have too, somehow Tony knew that.

Pillow cases were not the only wrapping for those overseas bundles. Some used cloth flour sacks . . . one hundred pounds . . . and bleached a couple of hundred times. Somehow they always remained a little stiff. Few families used them for actual pillow cases. They were all right for aprons and sheets but kind of scratchy on the face.

On the subject of used flour sacks, the guy from Little Falls (the biology professor) told of a very early experience he once had. His grand mother lived with his family and her room was upstairs toward the rear of the house. One Sunday morning, his mother told him to go upstairs to make sure 'nonna' was up . . . they were all going to go to an early Mass. The family was planning to go all the way to Utica for the feast and the procession of Sts. Cosmo & Damiano. It was going to be a big day for him and his three younger sisters.

He dutifully climbed the rear stair case and went to nonna's room. The door was ajar and he didn't rap on it, he just lightly pushed on it. It noiselessly swung open, and he looked into nonna's room. The boy's mouth dropped open, his eyes widen, he half gasped and quietly stepped back and hurried down the stairs.

His mother saw him return to the kitchen and asked, "Well??"

"She's up Mom, she's getting dressed", was his reply.

His mom squinted and looked suspiciously at him. "Are you all right??? Is something wrong??"

"Naw ma, everything is okay. I'm gonna go out on the front porch, okay?'

"All right . . . but don't get dirty!" she warned him.

The front screen door slammed behind him. He found a place on the glider and puffed out some air. He wanted to ventilate. He puffed again. He could not totally believe what he just saw!! Who would believe him?? He himself would not believe it if some one told him!!! WOW!!!

When the door quietly swung open in nonna's room, he saw her by the dresser, picking out clothes. She was barefooted; two thirds of her calves were showing, and she was wearing a flour sack as a night gown! She was smaller woman and needed only to cut a half a circle for her head and neck . . . and cut out the corners for her arms. The soon to become biology professor noted that the Gold Medal Flour Company of Milwaukee, Wisconsin in their own little way, contributed to his grandmother's not too extensive wardrobe.

Tony had no problem believing every word of that story. He wondered if she used the sacks for pillow cases. "Naw!!" he reasoned," . . . the kid would have seen them on the clothes line: further, the night gowns and personal underwear were always washed separate and apart from the others." A good story Tony thought to himself afterwards. He knew a hundred such women would have done the same thing, if they could fit into a hundred pound flour sack. Because Paulie lived a very short distance from where this reminiscing party was taking place, (maybe only a solid nine iron shot from here at their table) he mentioned his name. "Oh Yeah!!" said Ray Marashian, "he was my cousin."

"Really??" Tony said and then continued, "I didn't know you were Armenian!"

"Of course I am!!!" Ray said. And he was about to continue, when Tony snapped his fingers, then quickly made a child's gun with his hand and pointed it at Ray.

"I should have known . . ." Tony publicly admitting to a fifty year oversight/mistake, "Your last names ends with i-a-n just like his!!" What a revelation and all these many years (. . . How big of jerk are ya, anyway?? he thought to himself,) And then aloud, he said "Are you really his cousin??"

"Hey," Big Ray replied, "we were all cousins."

Tony wasn't sure as to how to interpret that answer. Were they cousins like the blacks call themselves 'brothers'?? Or was there blood there between Paulie and Ray? It would have been great if Paulie had a fistful of relatives. Maybe that haunting scene that surfaces sometimes in Tony's sad moods—mother and son leaning against an auditorium wall—alone, just shyly looking around, the boy avoiding eye contact—maybe that was just an isolated incident from a hundred years ago. Maybe, too, Paulie had a little party at home that afternoon, maybe.

No, you can't change the past by wishing something. They were Armenians fleeing to America to save their lives . . . (sometimes families would be separated). the Ottoman

Empire—a less known holocaust. Tony remembered again how Paulie lifted his gaze from somewhere off to the left of Tony's shoulder . . . looked Tony squarely and as never before, or since, or as deeply, and said, "I am Armenian!" That time it was Tony who looked away first.

It was time to go home. He ordered the cannoli's for his kids, stepped up to the pastry counter, paid the girl for the cannoli's and returned to the small circular table. Tony place a five dollar bill upon a little pile of money gathering in the center. The big men who sat at the small table and drank espresso from tiny cups, (sometimes occasionally stirring the coffee with tiny spoons), were done and making peace with the owner.

Tony caught Bob's eye and asked, "Is that enough??" Bob, who did not leave East Utica since his studies in Italy, did not answer aloud, he only jerked his head to the right, raised his right hand behind his left ear, as if giving absolution. The gesture indicate it was more than enough.

They said their good byes. Tony, with his neatly tied pastry box, (How do they tie the boxes so quickly?? . . . and snap the string . . . all in one motion?) got into his green pickup truck and went home. What a beautiful word—'home!!—almost as beautiful as family.

Epilogue

The Visitation
White Water Basin
Winter Fig Tree

Visitation at The Final Requiem

There is no more 'paging up' or 'paging down. We are simply going to click onto "File' and watch the menu drop in a heart beat. We'll navigate the cursor to "Save As", click onto it and then go on with life.

You know sometimes when you wake in the middle of the night . . . and you are kind of disoriented? you ask yourself . . . where am I? A second or two later you'll say, "Oh yeah . . . I'm at such and such and am safe!! You reach up, maybe pull the blanket over your shoulder, drive your nose deeper into the pillow, lazily breathe, inhale, maybe catch the scent of the shampoo you used just a few hours ago when you showered, and then have blessed repose in the form of a deep peaceful sleep warm and safe.

Or maybe sometimes you'll wake up, maybe after some "heavy drinking" and be disoriented, but it is not the same; you ask yourself a hundred questions that you can not for the life of you answer, "Who was I with? . . . where am I? . . . what did I do??? . . . shit!!! where the hell am I?? Can't get up now . . . don't think I could . . . where am I? The kids? The kids all right? Is the wife pissed off at ya ?? I don't know . . . where was I? What did I drink? Where did I eat??? What did I eat?? A restaurant . . . at home?? Who was I with?? Aw Jesus!!! Why can't I remember anything and think straight???

And you will fall back to sleep . . . eventually . . . but it is not the same restful sleep . . .

Sweet Jesus!!! Where the hell am I?? Where?

Hey, this looks like the parking lot at the rear of Peppie's . . . yeah . . . that's Mohawk Street . . . there's Bleecker . . . even in the dark I can make out the rear of Carmen's . . . to the left of Flihan's . . . Whaddam I doing here??? There's my truck . . . I gotta sit . . . pop the tail gate down sit on that . . . whadda i'm doing here . . . how did I get here . . . nobody is around . . . Look at those stars!! There must be a zillion of them . . . there used to be a big brownstone right here in this parking lot . . . Paulie used to live here when we were both in school . . . a long time ago . . . yeah a very long time ago . . . dangle your legs . . . feels kind of good . . . like when you were a kid . . . but how did I get here? . . . whadda I'm doing here? Nobody is around!!!

A vehicle is traveling north on Mohawk . . . zipped right through . . . he caught the light . . . look at him disappear into the darkness . . . up Mohawk . . .

Look at all those stars!!!

What the hell ? What made this tail gate bounce a little . . . like somebody else just got on? Paulie !!! you son of gun . . . how you doin??? You look like the kid that once told me about how hawks and geese fly . . . Remember?? . . . you didn't grow old at all!!! . . . no white hair . . . or bald spots . . . no fat gut. Look at him . . . just cocking his head and looking away . . . you never change huh Paulie??? That made him smile . . . Good . . . good old Paulie . . .

Boy look at those stars!!! . . . Hey Paulie . . . you want a shot of grappa??? . . . there is just a little bit left in the bottle . . . we drank most of it earlier . . . (I think) . . . and I ripped off coffee cups from Peppie's . . . I'll get them and we'll have a drink . . . what . . . you don't want any . . . ??? . . . I can tell by the look . . .

It's okay . . . I really don't want any myself . . . I drink too much . . . just ask my poor wife . . .

So tell me big guy . . . how you doin . . . ??? Hey! HEY! Wait a second . . . the guys told me you died!!! Are you dead? You're still not talkin Huh?? Just sitting there and rocking your head back and forth . . . not a yes not a no . . . okay . . . have it your way . . .

Hey Paulie . . . you ought to know . . . is there a heaven and is there a hell . . . ? Don't just sit there on my beautiful tail gate . . . swinging your legs and shrugging your shoulders . . . you know . . . but you won't tell me HUH?? . . . you know what I think Paulie? I think that there IS a heaven . . . and I think you are there . . . like Lazurus in the bosom of Abraham . . .

HA! Now I got your attention . . . you fi nally looked me in the eye . . . bout time . . .

You wanna know why I think that? Because guys like you . . . Fridone . . . Finnocchio . . . my cousin Antoinette, basically good people, loving people . . . geese that have to keep pumping their wings . . . just to stay in place and not fall back too far . . . go to heaven . . . and those that taunt and disrespect basically good people go straight to hell . . . shit heads like I am sometimes . . . I gotta get to heaven . . . if there is a heaven . . . I just gotta . . . good people are not junk!!! Right Paulie??? You are still not talking are you???

Know sumptin?? You haven't taken your eyes off me since I went on this little tirade . . . you are getting better with your eye contact Paulie . . .

Tell me Paul . . . is heaven like when I was a little kid? And when the four o'clock whistle would blow, I'd run up to the corner and watch and wait as a river of people streamed out of the mills . . . and finally spot my father . . . I can still see him . . . lunch pail in hand . . . crossing Kossuth . . . waving good bye to Don Alberto, breaking out in a big smile when he stopped me . . . he'd mess my hair . . . I'd ask him if he needed any help carrying the lunch pail . . . he'd hand it to me . . . and then would put his hand on my shoulder . . . and we'd walk down Catherine Street . . . up the alley way . . . and to our home . . . and be warm and safe and sure . . .

Ah . . . Ha !!!I gotta ya smiling huh???

Is that what heaven is like, Paulie? That kind of feeling?? How about playing on the floor with little empty torrone boxes . . . that became tanks or cars or a train . . . half hearing Ma singing softly . . . sitting by the kitchen window and under the clock with a rearing horse and a lasso twirling cowboy . . . patiently and diligently darning socks . . . it's gotta be like that Huh Paulie? . . . gotta be warm and safe, a protected home . . . right Paulie . . . ??

I'm on a roll Paulie . . . is it like waiting to hear the bells from the churches in snow covered Moscow peal joyously . . . loudly . . . right smack in the middle of an artillery barrage . . . or . . . all of sudden . . . the chorus comes in on the Ninth Symphony . . . there is HOPE . . . there's gotta be!!! Right Paulie??? Some kind of hope . . .

You know Paulie . . . I was not Jesus Christ growing up . . . whoring around . . . drinking . . . lying like a rug . . . I don't think I am any better as The Father (. . . as in the name of . . .) still drink too much . . . am moody . . . short tempered . . . cynical . . . I don't know . . . maybe I'll make a better Holy Ghost than a Father or a Son . . . I hope so . . . the Holy Ghost . . . like a pigeon hurled into a blue cloudless sky . . . wing tucked in for a second or two . . . then . . . and . . . then!!!! bursting open the wings and flying upward . . . and maybe gracefully circling . . .

You're looking at the stars again . . . huh??? . . . a beautiful night ain't it??

I drink too much . . . and Paul . . . to be honest with you . . . and looking back . . . I wasn't as respectful or sensitive to you when I could've been . . . I was junk . . . just another one of those shit heads that used to tease you . . . junk!!

What did you say??? I didn't hear ya . . . I'll get closer . . . say it again . . . will ya??

What??? A pillow with lace edging . . . I'm in my bed . . . what a dream . . . it was about Paulie . . . you remember . . . and about Ma and Pa . . . Catherine Street and the old brownstone . . . the alleyway . . . Donetta . . . and Fridone and Big Finnocchio . . . all of them . . . and remember Paulie won't talk in the dream . . . not till the very end when he finally did he say something . . . what the hell was it??? What did he finally say to me?? Damn it . . . I can't remember!!!

Later . . . much later . . . during the day . . . Tony finally remembered.

"Yes !!! Yes!!!" . . . it came to him . . . he made a fist with his right hand and waved it over his head and behind his ear . . . "yes!!! . . . Yes!!! that was it!!! *Dats* what he said!! JUNK!!!"

Spittoons . . . Tuscany cigars . . . Fridone and a Foresteri . . . metal/wire clothes hanger screwed into the backside of the bedroom door . . . Finnocchio and Bull Dog . . . fish on Fridays . . . Friday night baths . . . alley ways and stoops . . . used clothes lines . . . wrapped fig trees . . . fried chicken blood and gnumariedis . . . bare footed stout matrons walking in a procession . . . Miss Bailey and Mr. Luxs . . . menacing hawks . . . a pure white pigeon thrown forcefully into a cloudless pale blue sky . . . then bursting open it's wings . . . short quick flaps . . . then flying away . . . safe . . . without fear . . . in it's environment . . . Paulie told Tony: *"There is no such thing as junk."*

White Water Basin

She would place the fresh cut catalonia into an oval two gallon, painted white porcelain water basin.

The bundles of catalonia were tied in tight little circles and stood on end like soldiers at attention.

She would find a place for the basin somewhere on her two-wheeled pushcart.

Maybe between the cucumbers and tomatoes.

She then added about three inches of water into the basin.

And if you were to ask her why, she'd reply,

"To keep them alive."

And the kids all believed her . . .

Even though they knew the stems were cut from their roots.

Winter Fig Tree

Excerpt of previous correspondence to Robert Cimbalo

Page Down

Still on the dust jacket. I don't think you will mind, but I visualize your *Winter Fig Tree* painting dominating the back of the jacket. It is, I realize, a very personal thing (and I don't want to get corny on you), but to me and what I see (maybe "feel" would be a better word) in this painting is a combination of a requiem and a promise.

The promise is a reminder of the good things to come, the hope (la speranza) of fruit for your table, some shade from the restless hot August sun.

When the time comes to winterize a fig tree, in November or early December, and you find yourself trying to tie tight little square knots in pieces of "used clothesline" and your fingers are both numb and achy from the cold winter air and from the necessity of stuffing and wrapping, (dry fallen leaves, maybe some straw, a beat-up and old carpet, maybe even a good size piece of disregarded tar paper for a nearby construction site), junk, just junk, worthless stuff. That promise seems a long way off. A very long way off. Aah! But what you are really wrapping and stuffing and binding is a dream, *that Hope,* be it little or grand, which in time will soon reappear and in it's own magnificent way nourish you.

I love that painting. It talks to me and I try real hard to listen and I try even harder to understand.